I was vaguely aware of the presence of Max and the horses, but my heart and soul and body responded in uninhibited delight as Violet opened my dress and ran her fingers over my breasts. She buried her face against me, crooning and murmuring endearments. And then she stilled, as if by great effort, and pulled away, resting her head against the plump upholstery of the curved back of the sleigh. She found my hand under the robes and held it tightly.

"You are so much more than I reckoned on," she said softly. "I am behaving like a wanton child." She turned her face toward mine, her eyes sparkling in the cold moonlight. "Thoughts of you crowd all else from my mind and my eyes want only to look at you. I have been searching for you all of my life."

The impact of her words served to break away any lingering hesitance in me. I moved decisively, aggressive in a way that was unfamiliar but that I knew was somehow exactly proper for the moment. I took her in my arms, covering her face and neck with kisses, sliding farther under the robes as I raised her skirts . . .

About the Author

Dorothy Tell — born 11-23-39 — San Francisco, California.

Dot and Ruth, her partner of twenty-one years, live in Dallas, Texas. They both yearn for a time when aging and needful parents, loudly individuating adult children, and demanding jobs can be put on hold while they "boondock" for a while in the southern Arizona desert. It will be wonderful. No phones. No TV. Solar panels to run the laptop. And whole days when they can walk and hold hands and who knows . . . maybe they'll find some other like-minded crones out there and decide to stay forever.

Works by Dorothy Tell

Wilderness Trek	1990
Murder at Red Rook Ranch	1990
The Hallelujah Murders	1991
"Going Up" (a story in *The Erotic Naiad)*	1992
"Peaches" (a story in *The Romantic Naiad)*	1993
Certain Smiles	1994
Promises (Erotic Stories)	(Coming Soon)

CERTAIN SMILES

BY

DOROTHY TELL

The Naiad Press, Inc.
1994

Printed in the United States of America on acid-free paper
First Edition

Edited by Ann Klauda and Christine Cassidy
Cover design by Pat Tong and Bonnie Liss
   (Phoenix Graphics)
Typeset by Sandi Stancil

Library of Congress Cataloging-in-Publication Data

Tell, Dorothy, 1939–
   Certain smiles / by Dorothy Tell.
      p.   cm.
   ISBN 1-56280-066-3
   1. Lesbians—Fiction.   I. Title.
PS3570.E518C47   1994
813'.54—dc20

                                                     93-47339
                                                         CIP

*For Ruth — light of my life —
lover, partner, friend —
forever.*

Special Thanks:

To Ruth — whose unerring insight, shrewd criticism, and willingness to take part in "what-if" sessions are a vital part of any writing success I might ever achieve.

To J.R. and Emily — without whom this collection of stories would still be only items in a file labeled "Ideas" — my heartfelt gratitude for your friendship and assistance.

To Ann Klauda, Christine Cassidy, and K.V.F. — thank you for editorial skills, patience, and support.

Table of Contents

Table of Contents

Certain Smiles

Jo set up camp at her favorite table in her favorite bar, LIPS. Here in the company of "her" women, she was in her element. It was her haven, her real home, her safe harbor against the hateful world in which she worked every day. She shrugged off the pain of this particular day and willed herself to slip into the *attitude*. She watched the door and assessed each woman who entered.

Of course she did it without seeming to. She was good at it. Fifteen years of adult practice had eroded all the rough edges and left her with a pretty good eye for just the right woman — the one with that certain smile.

Jo had actually found this woman a number of times, bedded her often, and three or four times had even managed to convince her to hang around for a year or so. Jo was a handsome, soft butch with a new car, a good job — at least, until today she had had a good job — and she had no addictions. But "something" always happened. Try as she would, Jo couldn't make it last.

She sipped some seltzer water, moistening her lips so they would shine just right in the dim light. She really would've preferred a beer tonight, but she'd learned the hard way that even a little alcohol affected her judgment. Her mind kept turning back to the morning's meeting at work. It made her nervous and agitated, and she tried to think of something else — the evening's prospects — anything but face the decision she would soon have to make.

It was hard to believe she'd been laid off after sixteen years with the same company. Each day the torture of making herself fit into an alien mold. Each day making the supreme effort to remain in the stifling closet of her life. Pantyhose, power suits, company parties attended with gay men friends — and all for the promised prize of vested retirement.

But now all the rules were changing. The company was downsizing. Laying people off. Forcing early retirement for those who *could* retire. But they *were* offering a bit of a plum for those gutsy enough to grab it. If Jo dared, she could opt to receive all of her retirement fund money in one chunk instead of waiting until that far-off day when she would be fifty-five. Fourteen years. Fucking forever. But if she took it all now, how would she live when she *did* reach retirement age? And the worst of it was, she had to decide within the coming week. It was a one-time-only offer — act now or forget it for fourteen years.

Shit. She was *doing* it. She was *thinking* about it. She shook her head, as if movement would drive the problem away. She resumed her search for that certain smile.

Women lined the bar and crowded around the scarred pool table. Some of them were looking her way. Jo was tall and blond and rangy and good-looking in a Martina kind of way. Her gray eyes looked out from under heavy blond brows, over high cheekbones and a wide mobile mouth. All she would have to do was smile at most of the women who were looking her way, and her bed would be warm.

But she kept losing her place, sort of. Like reading the same words on a page over and over without knowing what they said. She shook her head again and put a little more concentration into this evening's installment of her lifelong search for that one certain woman, the one who would become Jo's happiness. The one who would smile that certain confident, sexy smile at her every day, forever and amen.

A shadow fell across the table and Jo looked up to find her best friend Nell leaning against the table. Nell was the bartender at LIPS and Jo's ex-lover. She didn't have The Smile, but she was steady and loyal and couldn't seem to ever quite fall *out* of love with Jo.

"Hey, babe." Jo grinned up at Nell. *"Que pasa?"*

Nell gestured toward the empty seat opposite Jo.

3

Jo nodded, catching a hint of nervous energy coming from Nell as her friend settled into the booth.

"How's it going, Jo? I've been watching you. You look a little down or distracted or something." Nell rested her chin on her folded hands in the winsome way that always tugged at Jo's heart. She looked closely at Jo with eyes so brown they seemed black in the darkened bar.

"Got your radar really tuned up, huh, babe?" Jo blotted beads of condensation from her water glass with a tortured paper napkin. "You always know, don't you?"

Nell sat quietly, apparently happy to have Jo's attention and to have her own assessment of Jo's behavior ratified.

Jo continued, "Yeah . . . I got laid off today." To her dismay, she heard her voice crack and go squeaky on her.

"Damn." Nell's eyes widened. "That's a helluva note. You've been there a long time."

"Yeah, but that doesn't count for much these days. Things are changing. They laid off Bertie from the mailroom, and he's been with Frankel's for twenty-seven years."

Nell sat quietly, seeming to mull over Jo's news. Then she shrugged and straightened abruptly. The nervous energy Jo had previously noted was again apparent in Nell's body language. "Well, I guess we're in the same canoe, Jodie Blond, and headed up shit creek without a paddle."

Jo was puzzled. "What are you talking about, Nell?"

"Marge is packing it in. Says she's getting too old

4

to run this place. She's put the bar up for sale and she and Andrea are moving to Florida ... and who knows *where* that leaves *me* ... guess you and me both got the ax today."

Jo glanced around the large, familiar room. She felt as if the second punch of a lethal combination had just caught her on the sternum. The breath seemed to leave her lungs in a rush. She looked at Nell and knew she ought to say something, but she was afraid the squeak would turn into a wail and her carefully guarded image would go the way of her stupid bloodsucking job.

Nell said, "I gotta go back to work — break's over. Why don't you stick around and help me clean up after closing time?" She touched Jo's hand lightly.

Jo nodded. She didn't really feel like entering the chase tonight. Some quiet, companionable time with Nell sounded good. She watched Nell make her way to the back of the bar. As behinds went, Nell had one of the great ones. Front wasn't too bad either. Life was a real joker — why couldn't Nell have been The Woman?

Even as the question entered Jo's mind, she knew the answer. The damned smile — or rather, the lack of it. Nell just didn't have it. Jo couldn't explain why that certain smile was so important to her or what she expected from women who had it, but she knew she would never stop looking for it. When she saw a woman's mouth lift at the corners and then — just like a slow-motion movie close-up — her upper lip would lift away from her teeth, her lower lip would curve down, and her eyes would telegraph that special communication, Jo was a goner. That smile always hit her just about heart-high with the force of an adrenalin injection, and she would go into full pursuit mode until it became clear that *this* woman wasn't The Woman.

Jo sat and toyed with her water glass, played a few games of pool, and helped a couple of friends to their car, making sure the sober half was behind the wheel. Soon, she noticed the lights were blinking for last call. The evening had dribbled away until she found herself alone with Nell.

Jo draped a barkeep's apron around her neck and efficiently wiped the tables and wrung out the mop in the utility room. She would miss this place. It was beginning to hurt like it had when she found out her favorite aunt had cancer. Even if LIPS remained as a lesbian bar, it wouldn't be the same. Jo knew all the routines. She'd even filled in as cashier when Marge was in the hospital.

Nell broke in on Jo's thoughts. "Wanna dance?"

Jo finished washing her hands and turned to face Nell. "Yeah, might as well. Might not get many more chances."

Nell switched on the music system, and a gravel-throated saxophone rode the beat of a conga drum while Jo and Nell glided across the dance floor. The combination of the heavy beat, which kept a steady pressure against Jo's tailbone, and Nell's lithe body pressed against hers soon gave Jo the mother of all horny hot-twats. A reckless energy seethed beneath her ribs and filled her groin.

Nell unbuttoned her shirt and let it slide from her freckled shoulders. Jo couldn't take her eyes off Nell's breasts. They swayed in front of her as Nell danced seductively backward and leaned against the pool table in a pose straight out of *Deneuve* magazine.

Nell said, "They say every butch's dream is to make it on a pool table. Wanna make your dreams all come true, Jo-baby?" Nell hiked her short skirt up to her hips and wiggled her behind onto the pool table. She lay back and spread her legs.

It wasn't The Smile, but just now the sight of Nell's naked pussy against the green felt of the pool table ranked as one of the most exciting things Jo had ever laid eyes on. She moved in closer and leaned against the ledge of the table, just over the side pocket.

Nell's legs closed around her and she let herself be drawn into a heated clinch. Soon Jo was prone on the table and her fingers were sliding in and out of Nell's pussy with a slow twist that was calculated to bring Nell to orgasm in another sixty seconds. Jo was well into the rhythm and her own breathing was ragged with passionate expectation.

They had fallen into an old, familiar routine. Soon after Nell came, she tugged Jo's jeans down to her knees and buried her face in the hot cleft of Jo's blond mound. Unable to grab hold of familiar bedposts, Jo wedged her hands against the sides of the table and was poised on the verge of a truly magnificent orgasm when a thought came crashing in on her. The orgasm quivered and retreated like a sneeze gone bad. Then it gathered again and shot from her like water from a fire hose. The wonderful new thought slipped through the waves of pleasure and rode them to a shimmering, hopeful place.

"Hey!" Jo shouted. "Hey —" She lifted her head

and glanced down at her crotch where Nell looked like a startled rabbit in a stand of winter grass. Jo sat up, grabbed Nell's arms, and pulled her up. "I just got this idea!"

"Well, that's perfectly obvious," said Nell as she tried to dry her cheeks and mouth on her forearm. "Spit it out, Jo . . . I don't know whether to be flattered or insulted. I mean, I either inspired you to have this great fucking idea or bored you so bad you tripped out to Oz."

Jo distractedly dried Nell's face with her shirttail. "No. I mean yes . . . I mean *listen!* " She leaped to her feet and stood with her jeans around her knees. She raised her arms like Rocky Balboa and gestured at the ceiling. "I can *buy* this place!" She sobered and looked at Nell. "I can get my retirement money early and buy LIPS for my very own."

Nell gave a shaky little grin as Jo pulled up her pants and began to hop around the room in an uncharacteristic manner, caressing the bar, hugging the jukebox, and kissing the cash register. They sat and talked and planned for hours and made love again just for "good measure."

That night was the beginning of Jo's great adventure. She barely felt her separation from the job that had been her main focus for so many years. She moved headlong into the blur of work it took to complete the deal that made her the new owner of LIPS — now renamed SMILES. With Nell's help, she closed the bar for a week and drove herself like a crazy woman to complete the repairs and minor changes she wanted to make. She and Nell were together every day and it only seemed natural to extend this togetherness to include the nights. The

8

more they worked together, the more Jo experienced a new respect and admiration for Nell. She had a new feeling for her that was hard to identify. But, whatever it was, it was good.

The day for the grand opening came all too soon. The bar was fully stocked, the pool table wore a new wine-colored felt cover, the plants were all misted, and Jo and Nell were spiffed up in new outfits. There was still a half-hour before the doors would open, so Jo seized the moment and sat for a while at her old favorite table. The past month was a blur. She was excited, scared, happy, and nervous. During the past weeks, the reality of what she had done had seemed to float just out of reach somewhere, jumping out at her at unexpected moments, pushing the breath from her lungs.

In a little more than a month, she had gone from passive Jo, lifer accountant at Frankel's Actuarials, to Jo, risk-taker and sole owner of a lesbian bar named SMILES. Had it really been just thirty-three days since she and Nell had baptized the pool table and the idea to buy the bar had exploded into her life?

It was good, though. For the first time in her life Jo was doing something *she* wanted to do. She was her own boss. It felt so goddamn good she wanted to fly around the room. She stood, full of enough nervous energy to become a burning bush. A burst of lesbian flame. She smiled at her private joke and had started across the room to help Nell go over the checklist when she looked up and caught sight of The Smile coming toward her.

That certain smile she had been chasing all her life was plastered ear to ear on the face of a tall, blond butch with laughing gray eyes and a bar towel slung over her shoulder. Jo stopped dead in her tracks and let the great tsunami of epiphany wash over her. *Of course,* she thought, as she looked at her reflection in the mirror. *That's it! It isn't something out there . . . it's something inside of me.*

She caught Nell around the waist and nuzzled her neck. She had never expected the smile search to end this way, but now she would have a lot more energy for other pursuits. Like making a happy life with Nell. She looked up again and grinned at her reflection. Yes! It was still there. A certain smile of her very own.

The Leather Shop

Ella felt the energy in the room change. Her partner Kate was slowly working up to something. She watched over the edge of her paper as Kate removed her glasses and placed them on the desk. With one hand she aligned them exactly with the edges of a yellow tablet and a pencil while she massaged the bridge of her nose.

"Ella . . ." Kate said.

"Hmmm?" Ella responded without digressing from her Sunday morning ritual of newspaper catch-up.

"Ella," Kate said sharply. "I think we need to talk about something."

Ella looked up and furrowed her brows. She closed the paper, folded it double, and placed it on the table beside her chair.

"Okay . . . what?"

"Do you realize that sex has become an item on our schedule?"

"And thank God for that." Ella's hand wandered toward the newspaper.

"No, Ella," Kate said. "I'm serious. Look." She tapped the tablet in front of her. "Here it is. *Sunday — Make time for intimacy.* It's parked here between *Newspaper* and *Fertilize houseplants* like some kind of maintenance reminder."

Ella tried not to smile. Kate was not trying to be funny. After fourteen years together, Ella knew when not to laugh. This was a definite *not.*

"What is it about that that bothers you?" Ella asked, using her very best pseudo-therapist inflection.

Kate raised one eyebrow. "Well. It certainly says something about the spontaneity of our extended stay here in lesbo-land." She ran a hand through her short brown curls. "We used to fall on each other like animals. Now we just fall on the bed. What's happened to us?"

Ella considered the question for a few seconds. It seemed to require just the right answer. "I don't think anything has happened to us. I think we're growing older. We're both thirty-six now — not twenty-two, just out of college. Our careers are demanding . . . and *dull,* God knows." Ella rose and walked to the window and stood looking out over the

12

back patio. "How the hell were we supposed to know at eighteen that four years of college accounting and fourteen years in careers of cost analysis and government auditing would turn us into bean-counting freaks who have to schedule weekly sex?" She turned to glare at Kate.

"Whoa, babycakes. Don't get your Fruit-of-the-Looms in a wad. I asked you first, remember?" Kate followed Ella to the window and embraced her. She wrapped long arms around her and nuzzled her neck, then stepped back, holding Ella at arm's length. "But, I just might have come up with an answer."

Ella stuck her chin out. "I'm not swallowing any more of those herbal concoctions, Kate."

"It's not herbs . . . not vitamins, yoga, tai chi, or lesbian romance novels." Kate grinned shyly. "I finally got around to ordering us a new vibrator after Wonder Wanda died — and they packed a catalogue in the box." She thrust a colorful booklet toward Ella.

Ella swallowed hard as she scanned the pages. Photo after photo of women in black leather and metal. Most of them had bare breasts and lots of mean-looking white teeth behind red lips. Clips, rings, and chains figured prominently, doubling as instruments which either held the outfits together or held the models prisoner, Ella wasn't quite sure which.

"Oh," Ella said, since Kate seemed to be waiting for her to react. "Uh . . . wow. They look like items from a masochist's Christmas list."

Kate pursed her lips like she always did when Ella refused to be serious.

"Okay, okay. Some of 'em look pretty sexy." Ella pointed at a picture of a woman in a shiny black PVC body suit which had cutouts for breasts and crotch. She turned another page, acutely conscious of Kate's scrutiny. That's when she saw an almost-nude woman wearing only a black garter belt and fishnet hose. "Whew." She felt her eyes widen. Now that really *was* sexy. She could certainly see how a red-blooded lesbian might get her libido jump-started if an outfit like that suddenly appeared in her partner's wardrobe.

Kate smiled, happy — Ella figured — now that she had gained Ella's full attention.

"I've been thinking about how lacking in adventure our love life is these days. I mean . . . I get it — you get it . . . then we take a nap. Same old routine." She smiled and held Kate's gaze with hers. "Satisfying and still wonderful, darling, after all these years," Kate said reassuringly. "But certainly nothing to write fem-lib essays about." Kate glanced coyly at Ella. "There's a leather shop across town. I think it might be fun to go shopping."

Ella felt the comfortable underpinnings of her orderly world tilt a little as she measured the determined sparkle in her lover's eye. She hitched up her Dockers and took a deep breath. Maybe a little walk on the wild side *was* what they needed to spice up their love life.

The next Friday morning, Ella found herself following that same determined lover into a store in a strip shopping center located in a part of town they had both agreed was career-death if they were recognized. They had chosen Friday because anyone who might know them would be working. Ella shrugged her shoulders forward, hunching herself into the smallest, least memorable persona she could fetch up. The big dark sunglasses across her nose made everything look very *film noir*.

For all Kate's obvious bravado and "healthy curiosity," she led the way down a leather-choked aisle like a normally honorable procurer who had been forced by the bad guys to pimp his sister. Ella tried not to giggle.

They were not approached by a salesperson. Ella was grateful for a while until she began to wonder if it was part of some bizarre punishment ritual. They wandered past stacks of camouflage underwear — men's *and* women's — and mannequins dressed like hooded executioners. They stood in front of glass display cabinets and perused gleaming chokers, handcuffs and metal-studded collars. They looked at other items of indeterminate purpose that were obviously designed to be worn over or around various body parts. Ella could tell that much by the size and strategic location of the holes in them.

In the back corner of the store, behind racks of Russian and German military uniforms, they found the section of garter belts, brassieres, corsets, bustiers and fishnet hose. Despite her nervousness, Ella felt a little giddy pinch in her groin as she eyed the mannequin perched on the cabinet corner. For some reason, that black garter belt, with all those long straps and old-fashioned hose-gripper snaps, set her heart to pounding. The way the hose tops looped down like naughty funeral bunting made her want to run her fingers under the sheer material.

Ella tugged at Kate's hip pocket and cleared her throat.

"Um ... what do you think of this?" She cut her eyes toward the mannequin.

Kate looked at Ella sharply, apparently trying to ascertain her seriousness. After a brief moment, she turned her attention to the mannequin.

"Well. It's very Madonna, isn't it?" She looked back at Ella and smiled. "For me or for you, dear?" She cocked a brow questioningly.

Now *that* was a new thought. It really hadn't occurred to Ella that *she* might be the one to wear it. She had been picturing long-legged Kate in the sexy outfit. She giggled nervously. "I guess I just assumed you would be the one to wear this stuff ... since you're the one who suggested we come here." She shifted her weight and rocked up on the balls of her feet as she waited for Kate's response.

Kate grinned. "Okay. I'll wear that for you if you'll wear something for me."

Ella had relaxed at the *okay* but felt her shoulders tense at the bargain Kate offered. She glanced at the many costumes around them. She was hesitant, but she nodded and made her mouth smile at Kate. After all, Kate might be having similar mental pictures of what *she* would like Ella to wear. The thought was unsettling, but wasn't that what they had discussed every morning for the past week? How they needed to climb out of their rut? To become *un*settled?

Kate grinned back at her with that sparkle again in her eye and turned toward the front of the store.

Ella turned to follow her and was startled to discover that they had been joined by a very tall, completely hairless man dressed in a prom dress and heels. He blotted his lipstick in the palm of one hand and then worked his hands together in a slow sensual gesture of expectant pleasure.

"May I help you, dahlings?" His voice was somehow reassuring as it flowed around them. Androgynous and friendly, with just the right mix of Judy Garland and Rod Stewart.

Ella stared at his smooth and completely denuded arms and hands. As he listened to whatever Kate was whispering, his hands and wrists moved in choreographed grace. Then, pointing in delighted animation toward the front of the store, he glided up the aisle like a model on a runway. He seemed totally oblivious to the effect his bald head was having on Ella. She felt like an idiot but she couldn't stop staring. What a magnificently eccentric and exotic human being he was.

The beautiful man and Kate stopped in front of a display of body harnesses. Ella gulped as she watched Kate's face light up when the man opened a locked cabinet and withdrew a tangled mass of black straps fastened together with O-rings. At a nod from Kate, he lifted the contraption over Ella's head and lowered it, expertly adjusting the straps until they lay in orderly radial directions across her shoulders, chest, and torso. Before she could object he had plopped a black police hat on her head and turned her to face the mirror. The effect was a stunning transformation from Ella, slightly butchy career dyke, to Ella, closet dominatrix.

Dominella.

Ella caught sight of Kate's expression in the mirror. She looked like a kid in line for her first ride on the *Runaway Mine Train.*

Ella examined her own reflection. She was still the same person. Nothing there had changed. Same blond ponytail, same blue eyes behind the Foster Grants, but the costume added something. It evoked images of strength and authority and some kind of no-no feeling in the pit of her stomach. She smiled at her thoughts and let herself be turned around again by the graceful man.

"Dahling," he was saying to Kate. "You *know* this is designed to be worn over bare skin ... nothing between your masterful woman and these straps but a delicate sheen of perspiration."

Ella watched Kate for her reaction to this information. She wasn't disappointed. Kate's pink tongue was visibly tracking the underside of her lips as her hand went into her pocket for her wallet. She withdrew it, then stopped and looked at Ella. "You okay with this, hon?"

Ella felt her back straighten as she rocked up on the balls of her feet and turned to look once more at the mirror. She flexed her shoulder and neck muscles, watching with interest as her Dominella reflection lipped a wicked grin at Kate and nodded. "Sure," she said, "Why not? Whatever turns you on."

She felt an electric thrill run from her groin down to the backs of both knees as she watched Kate's face grow sober, then light up again. That giddy thrill belonged in the past. She remembered it from their dorm days at college, when she and Kate would cut class and stay in bed all day, chancing ruinous discovery and disgrace but completely unable to stay away from each other.

A mood of expectant excitement filled Ella as they paid for their purchases and slunk back to the car like two kids with a book of matches and half a cigar. They got in, looked at each other, and broke into nervous giggles.

Ella spoke first. "Would you do something for me, Kate? Something special?"

"Well, sure, hon. I mean . . . I guess so." Kate's face suddenly sobered as she glanced at the gaudy bags that held their purchases. "I mean . . . well, what is it you want me to do? This is new territory. Maybe we'd better discuss this whole costume idea and set up some guidelines. Some rules . . ."

"You mean add it to our schedule?" Ella prodded Kate. "Under some category like *Liberate Libido?*"

Kate grinned good-naturedly. "We sure know how we are, don't we?" She made her face serious. "C'mon. Tell me what you want me to do. I may actually have a spontaneous bone left in my body. I think I felt it loosen up back there when that marvelous creature called you my masterful woman."

Ella remembered that the same feeling had poked her in the twat along about that same time. She looked at Kate, picturing exactly how she would look in the black lace garter belt and hose. "Let's go in the Mickey D restroom over there and try on our new stuff."

"Omigod," Kate said. "We can't do *that!* In *McDonald's* with *children* and smelly little babies and their moms banging around on the *changing table*? Oh *gag* . . .Oh no, I don't think so, Ella."

"Well, get a grip, Kate. We're not going in there to flash anyone. We'll each one go in a stall and put our new power-undies on, put our clothes back on over them, and leave. No one will know we've done anything radical. Er, radical for us, that is. Then we can just leave and go for a walk in that park across the street." She took Kate's hand. "Nothing fancy — just two lezzies out for a walk on the wild side of town. No one's going to know us over here." She stopped, realizing her voice had taken on a pleading note. "Might be fun. You know. Just knowing what each other was wearing . . . underneath, I mean, with no panties and all."

Kate looked at Ella with a hint of shyness. "Well . . . I guess it wouldn't hurt anything." She reached for the door handle. "Okay. Let's give it a shot."

Twenty minutes later, they were sitting on a white wrought-iron bench by a duck pond like two fourth-graders discussing their first menstrual periods. Shy, excited, proud, embarrassed, uncomfortable, and chafing in places they didn't know they had.

"Ella," Kate ventured. "I really don't think anyone in Mickey D's could hear you clanking."

"Well, *I* could hear it. I feel like Robo-dyke." She grinned at Kate. "Let's go in that restroom and get back to normal. I'm beginning to get that promised 'sheen of perspiration' and it's galling my upper thighs."

Kate nodded in agreement, obviously stifling an

urge to laugh. She rose and strode off toward the sandstone building marked. *Women.* Ella walked behind her, glancing around to assure herself that they had the area mostly to themselves. She saw Kate stop for a moment, take a hobbling step forward then pull up short. Her shoulders were shaking and Ella was pretty sure it was silent laughter. This was definitely not a time for the giggles.

She drew even with Kate and touched her shoulder. "You okay?"

"Hoooooo — hoo — hoo." Kate gasped, doubling over, tears of laughter streaming down her face. "My hose snappers are — hoo-hoo — hung up. I can't move — hah ha hoooo."

Ella looked at Kate in amazement. "Do you expect me to *carry* you into the restroom? Can't you walk at all?" Ella felt her resistance give way to glee that soon took over her body like an alien force. "Oh, God, Kate. Don't fall down. Try to make it in there and I'll get you unhooked."

Kate hopped toward the restroom as if her legs were joined to each other at the knee. She made it to the doorway and jigged her way inside, followed closely by an almost hysterical Ella.

They shut the door, locked it, and both of them slid down the wall to sit on the clean tile floor, legs out in front of them, laughing like it was three A.M. on the second morning of a two-day junior-high slumber party.

Ella finally got her wind and began to pull down Kate's slacks. She unhooked the offending snaps and began to *look* at her lover. Her hiccups stopped abruptly. She removed her shirt and slid it under

21

Kate's bottom. Kate lay back, relaxed from laughing, arms akimbo, with her slacks about her knees. The black lace garter belt looked like velvet soot against her white nakedness. Her dark pubic mound made a perfect heart-shape above her cream-colored thighs.

Ella felt desire flood through her. A powerful physical hunger made itself known in a rush of blood to her groin. She was panting with passion and excitement. Her hand flashed out and settled against Kate's lower abdomen. She ran the fingers of her other hand beneath the top of the fishnet hose. Kate's eyes flew open in surprise.

Ella couldn't stop herself. She cradled Kate with one strong arm and explored Kate's moist labia with her fingers. She found Kate's mouth and kissed her, increasing the pressure of her fingers on Kate's clitoris as their kiss grew more passionate. Kate moaned against Ella's mouth and began to make movements with her hips that meant she was on the verge of orgasm, as Ella knew from long experience.

Ella was overcome with the strangeness of the moment — of where they were, what they were wearing, and *migod,* what they were doing on the floor of a public restroom. Something inside her broke free and cavorted naked and grinning, baring its little fanny to the wind and chasing butterflies. Kate had barely come to orgasm and was still clenching her legs together when Ella quickly stepped out of her Dockers and stood over Kate, spreading her pussy lips so Kate could see the narrow silver chain glinting against the pinkness. Her breasts, framed by the straps of the leather harness, jutted out proudly. Her nipples were hard and ached to be touched.

Kate wasted no time. Her eyes opened wide and dark. She found the chain between Ella's legs and gently pulled her down. Ella felt Kate move the chain aside and place her tongue against her twitching clitoris. Then Kate wrapped her arms around Ella and pulled her forward and began to work the tongue-magic that Ella loved so well.

Ella came with such force that she thought she would stop breathing. Again and again Kate's tongue and mouth made her jerk like a puppet on a string.

They had probably been in the restroom for less than ten minutes, yet both of them had had explosive orgasms and they were still panting.

They looked at each other.

"What happened?" Kate asked as she dressed, more careful this time with the garter-belt snaps as she pulled up her slacks.

"I'm not sure, sugar ... but I think you and I just climbed out of our rut." Ella grinned as she stepped into her Dockers and tugged them up, buttoning them over the harness straps.

"Honey," Kate said, as she helped Ella button her shirt. "I haven't felt like this in years. You think it'll last?"

"Probably." Ella thoughtfully observed her frazzled reflection in the buffed metal mirror. "Don't know about you, but I don't think *I'm* gonna need to put certain reminders on our to-do list from here on."

"Oh, honey. Me too." Kate got a faraway look in her eye. "C'mon. Let's get home. I think I've got a pair of pumps that'll be a knockout with these hose ... and a gangster hat ... got one of those somewhere, too."

They left the restroom arm in arm. Robo-dyke

and the Material Girl, grown-up champions of that old childhood game, dress-up.

Maybe that was it, Ella thought. It was her little-girl self, loose and giggling once again. Let out of her stuffy adult closet to play slippy-slidey in the girl's restroom with Marva Ann, her best-friend-in-the-whole-world from second grade.

Well, whatever it was, Ella intended to make playtime a priority on her mental list from now on. She *liked* it.

And so did Dominella.

The Book Club

Janet held the book out away from her body and turned it around to read the blurbs on the back cover. She could hardly believe that her book club had knowingly chosen this novel for the next meeting. She read every word on the book jacket and was satisfied that you could *not* tell from the cover that the book was about a woman doctor and her lesbian lover. She had assumed the doctor in the title was a man. After all, Janet was heterosexual, and she supposed everyone else in the club was too.

Repressed though, she admitted to herself. *I am repressed.*

The damned book was making her uncomfortable. She just might not finish it after all. She could feel her face heat up in a blush. How could she possibly sit in a roomful of men and women and listen to a review and discussion about professional lesbians? She almost smiled as she wondered if they ranked themselves like tennis players? Were there lesbians of amateur status? Lesbian tournaments maybe?

Janet marked her place with the needlepoint bookmark that her roommate Gina had given her two Christmases ago. She tugged the silken cord taut, closed the book, and carefully placed it face down on the reading table beside her chair.

Maybe this book club was not a good idea after all. Uncomfortable subjects made Janet think. And thinking made her uneasy. It was best just to keep one's mind on safe subjects like the planned purchase of an almost-new Toyota Tercel, or her job, or on books with two sexes on their covers.

She jumped with a guilty start when she heard Gina's key in the door. Her hand covered the book and quickly slid it out of sight between the arm and the cushion of her overstuffed chair. Gina burst in, smiling and talking and filling up the room with her bigness. That's the way Janet had come to privately describe Gina's bubbly personality and round full body. Gina filled all the corners and unlit spaces in Janet's life like the light from a sturdy and stalwart beacon.

"Those kids." Gina sighed and plopped herself into her chair on the other side of the reading table. "I can't believe my sister wants another one. She'll have four kids under six years old after the new one comes."

Janet admired Gina for helping her sister and brother-in-law by baby-sitting every Thursday night. Gina's attachment to her large noisy family was just one more reason Janet gave herself for being so comfortable about the life she shared with Gina. Janet had only her mother, who carped constantly. *Why* didn't she get out more? *Why* didn't she sign up for a singles club or *do* something with herself? As if her self were some garment to be remade at will.

Shyness was as much a part of Janet's nature as her height. She couldn't escape the fact that she was taller than most men and that her features, though not unpleasant, were far from beautiful. Her chin and jaw were strong and her clear blue eyes looked at the world from beneath pale, thick brows which her mother had finally given up trying to get Janet to color and pluck into a more manageable shape. Her thick lashes were almost blond and, unless she forced herself to apply mascara to them, they seemed not to be there at all, giving her face a surprised look.

She realized Gina had asked her a question, because Gina was quiet and looking at her quizzically.

"What?" Janet felt her face warm up. Blushes were another cross she bore with resignation. Her fair skin was an unerring emotional barometer for the world to read at will. "I'm sorry. What did you ask me?"

Gina shook her head good-naturedly. "I *said*, what new book did your club choose for this month?"

In Janet's imagination the offending book glowed against her leg like E.T.'s heart as she stumbled over the lie she was making up. "Some political thing I didn't care about. You know — written by some man up in New York about how we Southern women have messed up our male children." *My God, she thought. When would her tongue stop?*

"Oh, well. They all can't be fun, I suppose." Gina heaved herself from the chair. "Tomorrow's a workday and those kids gave me a headache. See you in the morning." She trudged toward her bedroom, and the room seemed suddenly darker. Except, Janet thought, for the light from the damned book. She felt the book's weight against her leg and experienced an unaccountable feeling of guilty chagrin.

She waited until she heard Gina's bedsprings creak before she reopened the book. The book drew her the way Gina said chocolates in the cupboard sang to *her*. She knew she shouldn't enjoy the story, but she read far into the night and finally went to bed only because her eyes wouldn't stay open any longer.

Though she was tired, she slept lightly and woke at every traffic sound from the streets below. And every time she woke, the story was there in the front of her mind, playing in Technicolor like a forbidden movie that wouldn't shut off.

She finally rose and took a shower before the alarm went off. She dared not take the book to work. Someone on the bus might get a glimpse of it and know what it was about. Or worse — someone at work might see it. So she hid it under the cushion of her chair and left for the bus stop. As she closed the door, she heard Gina's alarm go off for the first of the usual three times it would blast rock music at Gina before she would get up and drink her half of the coffee Janet always left for her.

Janet caught the bus, as usual, and rode to work among the crowd of familiar strangers. She entered her office building, climbed the four flights of stairs for her daily exercise, and then sat at her same orderly desk — as usual. But Janet didn't feel as she usually felt. She had the odd feeling she was wearing the wrong shoes or had a run in her hose or had forgotten to fix her hair. She was somehow out of sync with the reality of her mundane existence, as if she were watching a movie where the actors' lip movements were slightly ahead of or behind the soundtrack.

She was annoyed. She didn't like being constantly aware of her every action. She wanted to be lost in routine, to feel the dreamy passing of time at a distance, rather than being so damned aware of the world around her.

And of herself. She could feel the constant heat of a blush on her neck as she went through her daily routine.

Lunchtime finally arrived and she welcomed the chance to get out of the confining office for an hour. She hurried out into the bright, cool, Indian-summer air and walked to the little park down the block. She sat on a cement bench and shared her peanut-butter sandwich with the birds. She chided herself for not bringing a book.

The book.

The story of the two women claimed Janet's full attention as she let herself remember it. The writer was good and the tension was skillfully built as the story unfolded. The busy doctor had never really thought about the source of her pervasive melancholy until she had gone to a conference in another city and met a psychiatrist who was there to give a paper. The two women had met for lunch after the lecture and never left each other's company for the rest of the conference.

Janet's heartbeat quickened. She could hear it in her ears and feel it pulse in her neck as her out-of-control imagination projected the women in the story into what would surely be the consummation of their growing attraction for each other. She imagined that they made love together. She could see them naked in bed, touching each other as a man and woman did.

Unaccountably, Janet's throat constricted and she felt tears well up and trickle down her cheek. She rubbed away the wetness and realized she was still holding her half-eaten sandwich. She flung it to the grass, startling the birds gathered around her bench, and rose with more energy than she felt. She circled the block three times, walking fast, swinging her arms, hoping to clear her thoughts and bring her emotions into check.

The rest of the day was a trial for her. Tears seemed to be always on the verge of breaking loose, and only with great effort did she manage to concentrate. She vowed to keep her mind on the things she did want and off the things she did not want. It vaguely occurred to her, somewhere on the outer edges of conscious thought, that the things she did *not* want were not at all clear. She knew, however, that she didn't want to cry or feel her heart in her throat all the time. Janet marshaled her thoughts into the narrow focus of the trips she and Gina would take when Janet had saved enough money for the "new" car.

They would go to the beach, to the across town little theaters where all the best new plays were staged, and upstate and beyond when the "fall colors" motoring trips began. Her heart hummed with happy expectation and peaceful ease as her mental machinery did its work and the afternoon passed. By the time she boarded the bus for home, she had forgotten the morning's agitation. It was not until she sat in her reading chair that evening that she remembered the book.

She felt its hard edges beneath the cushion as she bent forward to remove her shoes. It was Friday night, Gina's turn to cook supper. Janet was looking forward to it, but the kitchen was dark and there were no cooking smells coming from anywhere, including the microwave. She checked, just to be sure. It wasn't like Gina to shirk a responsibility.

Concerned, Janet knocked on Gina's bedroom door. She heard a muffled, "C'mon in. I'm in bed."

Janet opened the door cautiously. Gina was indeed in the bed and she looked terrible. The crease between her brows signaled the secondary phase of one of Gina's legendary three-day headaches.

"I'm sorry, Jan . . . about supper." Gina shielded her eyes from the light coming into the room. "I didn't go in to work today. I've been in bed all day."

Janet swallowed her disappointment and said cheerily, "I don't mind. I'll just open a can of soup." She closed the door gently and headed straight for the book. If Gina was going to spend the evening in bed, it would give Janet time to finish the damned book and put it out of her mind. She changed into her pajamas, took the book and two apples into her bedroom, and closed the door.

The next morning Janet awoke to the kitchen sounds of Gina making breakfast. Shafts of sunlight streamed into the room between the slats of the blinds, catching dust motes in a sparkling dance. Janet turned onto her stomach, snuggled down between the covers, and stretched luxuriously.

As her hand brushed the book, guilty memories of furtive masturbation came to her in a rush.

She had finished the story in such a consuming heat that she had quickly brought herself to orgasm with the smooth handle of her favorite hairbrush. A blush ran the whole length of her body when she thought of her purely physical reaction to the book's climactic love scene. She had felt her own wetness as the two women in the story finally kissed and fell into bed. Janet's own explosive orgasm had shocked her. She had never gotten "it" exactly that way before. Her usual habit was to do it in the shower with the spurting force of the removable shower head as the sole stimulus for her necessary sexual release.

But this time she had touched her breasts, exploring them as if they belonged to someone else. She remembered how she had rubbed and pinched her nipples, caressing them, guiltily feeling their weight against her hand, the hard nipples prominent against her sensitive palm.

Janet tried to wrangle her thoughts into some other channel as she felt her clitoris growing hard and a clamoring ache grow in her lower abdomen. She climbed from bed and headed for the shower. Wonderful smells of baking blueberry muffins made her mouth water and she smiled at Gina's off-key humming.

Saturday morning was her favorite time of the week. She and Gina always had breakfast together on that day.

"Breakfast in ten minutes," Gina called down the hall.

" 'Kay. Be right there."

She showered in record time, paying special attention to make sure her body was fresh and clean, free of any hint of her nocturnal activities. She shampooed her hair three times, as if a shining head could somehow hide the guilty excitement below her waist.

Gina was already buttering her second muffin when Janet sat down across from her. Gina's ample body filled her clinging robe. One round arm rested beside her full middle. She grasped a buttery muffin with one hand and held a cup of steaming tea to her mouth with the other. She looked up at Janet and then quickly lowered her gaze to regard her teacup. She said nothing, pursing her lips and blowing softly at the hot tea.

"You seem better this morning," Janet ventured, trying desperately to think of nothing at all, since she couldn't seem to stop thinking about what she did *not* want.

"Yeah." Gina looked at her for a second, then averted her eyes again. "I think I just needed a do-nothing day at home. You know — without kids or bosses or telephones or deadlines."

"Mm-hmm," Janet mumbled, her mouth full of warm blueberry muffin. She washed it down with tea and realized Gina was quieter than usual. She wasn't chattering at full tilt and telling funny stories about baby-sitting the "tribe" or joking about what happened around the office water cooler. Maybe the headache was still bothering her.

Then Janet realized that *she* was also being quieter than usual. She noticed Gina looking at her in a new way, with a tiny little grin hovering around the corners of her mouth. Like she did when she had a secret.

Janet sat back and cleared her throat. "So . . . Gina. What's new at the job-from-hell? Are you still going to those computer-training classes?"

Gina rolled her eyes, indicating, Janet supposed, that things were still pretty much the same. Well. This was really going great. She was still searching for something else to say when Gina said, "Sometimes you can learn more by taking a day off." She gazed at Janet soberly.

Janet's heart skipped a beat and her stomach bottomed out as her usual paranoia made an appearance. She suddenly knew exactly what was wrong with her friend. Gina had found that damned book. *That* was it. She had probably read it and now she was going to tell Janet that she needed to find herself a new roommate, that she didn't want anything to do with someone who read dangerous trash like that and then *lied* about it.

Janet looked at her hands. She knew she had to say something. She struggled and somehow her tongue said exactly what her heart was wondering, rather than the garbage her mind was cranking out. "What did you learn, Gina?"

Gina put her unfinished muffin on the plate and slowly licked the crumbs from her fingers. Her pink tongue darted out of her mouth, efficiently gathering every last morsel from her plump fingers. She dried her hands on a napkin and took so long to answer that Janet's tinnitus rang in her ears like a cloud of summer cicadas.

"I learned that some people's happiness is different from everyone else's. And that doesn't make it wrong . . . just different."

Okay, okay. What did that mean?

Gina looked straight into Janet's eyes and continued. "I also learned that when people want something, they have to take a chance on getting it . . . they have to take a risk."

Oh, boy, here it comes, thought Janet. Now comes the part where she says she has to go off on her own on some damned adventure. Somewhere without clunky old shy Janet klutzing up the landscape and scaring all the eligible men away.

"Janet. Do you have *desires?* "

Janet's lungs stopped working.

Gina went on, "Not just goals. Not just buying your car or getting a raise." She looked at Janet searchingly, obviously waiting for an answer.

"Well, yeah," Janet croaked out. "I have things I want." She crossed her arms over her middle and sat up straighter.

"This is going nowhere," Gina muttered. "Maybe I asked the wrong questions. Maybe I should have asked you what you *don't* want. You know, how you're always telling me to keep my mind on the things I do want and off the things I don't want. Well, what are the things you tell yourself you *don't* want? What are you running away from?"

Janet felt the first tear escape and run down her cheek. It was obvious. Gina had read the book and now Janet's whole life would change as a result. She didn't know how to answer Gina's question. How could she possibly articulate what was only just now forming in her consciousness? The real answer was that it wasn't what she didn't want. It was what she didn't *want* to want.

The discovery reverberated like a ringing gong behind her eyes. It pounded in her ears like storm-driven surf. She dropped her face into her hands. Between her fingers she let the truth leak out in short painful sentences. "I want more from you than I have a right to ask. I'm sorry. I don't think I knew it myself until you asked me." She kept her eyes on her plate, unable to look at Gina.

"Why do you think I asked you?"

Janet was acutely aware that Gina had risen and was rounding the table, her blue robe glowing in the sun as she stood by Janet's side.

"I *said*, why do you think I *asked* you?"

Janet felt Gina's fingers under her chin, forcing her to look up. Gina's eyes were flashing and her cheeks had reddened as she held Janet's chin up.

With a rush of emotion so strong it almost left her faint, Janet realized exactly the meaning of the question that hung in the air like smoke from summer fireworks. She rose on legs suddenly strong with decision and pulled Gina close in a gentle but determined embrace. As Gina's full mouth pressed against hers and they shared their first kiss, Janet smiled against Gina's lips. She remembered the scene in the book and felt her blood quicken at what she knew would soon be a similar scene in her own life.

Finding Her Voice

Lillian Barry relaxed in her daily bath. Rather, she tried to relax. The hour was quiet and early, just the way she preferred. No noise, no music, no singing, no voices. Except for her own thoughts, which yipped inside her head like so many rowdy schoolgirls. Try as she might, peace would not come.

She slid farther down into the warm sudsy water, down until it lapped at her earlobes. The heat relaxed her body, if not her tortured mind, and her hands began to explore that hungry place below. Her legs parted until her knees rested against the sides of the tub. She reached up, found the long rubber tube of the hand-held shower attachment, and applied its spurting face directly to her clitoris.

Her clit leaped and danced under the pressing stream of water. Orgasm exploded from her groin and shot down her legs. She leaned her head back against the shocking cold of the tub rim and sighed as her heart pounded against her ribs. She moved the showerhead to and fro until she once more came to orgasm.

Then again and again and again — until her body shuddered and water sloshed in wavelets over the sides of the tub. Her heart thundered until she feared she might die. Finally, exhausted from the orgy of release and chilled from the cooling water, she stepped from the tub and studied her reflection in a large ornate mirror as she roughly toweled her still-trembling body.

Her thick black hair hung in damp ringlets against her white shoulders. Her dark amber eyes were large and liquid, and of late were underscored by the telltale dark puffiness of too little sleep.

Lillian liked to look at her nakedness. She knew why men wanted her. It thrilled her to watch as she moved her hands over her heavy, pink-nippled breasts. She turned this way and that to admire her slim waist and womanly hips. She stood hipshot, weight on one foot, bending her free leg at the knee, to better appreciate the shapeliness of her slender knees and ankles.

She sighed again and carefully draped the towel over a rack to dry. She powdered and perfumed her body with care. The lilac scent of White Shoulders sent little thrills down her spine.

I'm a fool, she thought. *I'm acting as if I were preparing for a date ... not just another day of singing classes.*

She caught her own eye in the mirror. "What is the *matter* with me?" she cried at her reflection.

But she knew what the matter was. She knew it very well. The *matter* was Valencia Maria de los Angeles Garza. The twenty-four-year-old only daughter of one of the wealthiest and most influential families in the valley. Garza Citrus was one of the world's largest grapefruit growers and Domingo Garza, father of Valencia and her four brothers, was a legend in the fertile Texas Valley. A legend who struck terror in the heart of Miss Lillian Barry, who had been employed to do the technically impossible and coax his darling Val's contralto growl into a coloratura soprano like that possessed by his equally darling wife, Olivia.

Lillian shook her head impatiently, chasing from her mind the powerful image of Domingo Garza. Lillian's task was to help Val Garza find her voice and she would do it. She was filled with happy expectation as thoughts of the girl filled her mind. Girl? Not really so much younger than Lillian's own thirty-one years ... but so effervescent and carefree with her teasing green eyes and blond hair worn in a girlish soccer bob.

Lillian had barely finished dressing and applying her makeup when a determined thumping announced that Val was early for her lesson. Her heart raced as she opened the door.

"Good morning, Lillian," said Val Garza as she strode into the room, her long legs clad in riding boots and jodhpurs. Her white shirt was open at the collar, each sleeve rolled to the elbow. The tan of her muscular forearms was complemented by the brightness of the fine cotton shirt. Her smile dazzled Lillian and her moss-green eyes sparked with energy as she moved toward the piano where the lesson would take place.

Lillian willed her tongue to work. "And good morning to you, Val." She joined Val by the piano bench. "Have you been practicing your breathing?"

Val nodded, smiling as if amused by something Lillian had either done or said.

"Val, I've been thinking about some exercises that might loosen you up a little." Lillian waited until she received a slight nod from Val before she went on. "Remember we discussed how to stand?" She sat on the piano bench and placed her fingers on the keys. She thought she could feel the warmth radiating from Val's body when she turned to look at her.

Val ran a hand through her hair as though frustrated at some failure. "I can't seem to get it right." She turned to Lillian, her palms upturned, pleading. "Can you show me again?" She looked down, her green eyes brimming with a reckless mischief. "Like you did last time?"

Lillian felt her heart lurch in her chest. She rose slowly from the bench and stood facing the tall young woman. She wanted to look at her but she dared not raise her eyes. She couldn't be sure her agitation would remain hidden. She began her instruction by rote. "Weight on your toes — heels slightly elevated. Like preparing to dive from a springboard . . . tuck your buttocks in . . . now stand tall — make the tallest spine you can make."

She stepped to one side and put two fingers against the back of Val's neck. "Here — let your head rest exactly on your spine. There should be no restrictions from your groin up to your throat. Clear lungs, clear passageway for the voice . . . open from diaphragm to the top of your head. Now — below the waist, use the same muscles for singing that you would use for gripping your horse's saddle."

Lillian could feel her face brighten with a blush as the words tumbled out. She placed her hand flat against Val's abdomen. "Here — breathe here, not with your nose . . . Now — concentrate on your instrument, your *voice*. Give me the scales, single sounds please —"

Val boomed out the first syllables, sounding very much like an effeminate foghorn.

"Concentrate on the tonal quality of your vowels — use vigorous lip action for consonants." Lillian knew in a flash what was about to happen. She saw Val's full lips close over the consonant and widen as the vowel sound came out. She watched the corners of Val's mouth turn up into a tiny grin as she covered Lillian's hand on her abdomen with her own. Val's face came closer and closer until she pressed her lips lightly to Lillian's.

Lillian wanted to resist, knew she *must* stop. But a fire spread through her. The astonishing knowledge that she was being kissed on the lips — passionately — by a *woman* sent a heated message to every sensitive area of her body. She felt herself responding, leaning into the kiss, hungry for more sensation, more feeling. Above her growing passion, in the clearness of lucid thought, was the sure knowledge that she would have to leave the valley.

She could not stay. Not after this. For all its vast fields, the valley was just like a small town. She had betrayed the community's trust in her. If she did not leave on her own, they would drive her away.

Then Val pulled away from her, still tightly holding her hand, pulling her toward the bedroom. Lillian walked on wooden feet, drawn like a damp-winged moth to the lesbian flame of Valencia Maria de los Angeles Garza.

She began to realize she was being seduced. Perhaps Val had never intended any other outcome to their weekly sessions. She *knew* this was not the first time for Val, could feel it in the way Val touched her. Val had gone away to Texas A&M and learned about more things than agriculture. She efficiently undressed Lillian, though she herself remained fully clothed. She was a practiced lover. She played the strings of the harp which had been Lillian until a single note filled the room. The sound of pleasure rushing past O-shaped lips and thrumming along every vein and muscle.

When the waves of Lillian's explosive orgasm had ebbed enough for her to speak, she began, "Val, I — I'm not sorry. You are so powerful. But this mustn't ever happen again."

Val stood and looked calmly at her. "Why not?" She unbuttoned her shirt and pulled it back over her shoulders. As if Lillian hadn't spoken at all, she loosened her pants, sat on the bed, and removed her boots.

Lillian watched, spellbound, as Val stripped her trousers off and stood naked before her, splendid in her tawny beauty, powerful strength apparent in her wide shoulders and muscled back. But she was completely mesmerized by the sight of Val's breasts. The nipples were pale, only a little darker than her silky skin, and the surrounding aureoles were wide and soft-looking.

Lillian felt her lips once more form a circle as a long sigh escaped. "Ooooohh," she crooned as her gaze dipped to drink in the totally naked surface of Val's shaven vulva. "There's no . . . you have no —"

"Yes." Val placed both hands over herself, slowly caressing the pale, plump lips as she spoke. "I like it this way." She walked closer to where Lillian lay on the bed until she stood mere inches from Lillian's face. "Tell me, *cantante*, what do you think of it?"

Lillian tried to speak but all that came out was a low moan. Speechless for the first time in her life, she looked up into the face of the woman who had stolen her heart.

"Can't talk, hey?" Val grinned, dimples bracketing her white teeth. "Can you show me, then?"

Lillian reached out, tentative at first and trailed her fingers lightly over the forbidden delta. Then her arms went around Val's hips and she pulled her forward, nuzzling her mouth against the cleft mound. She twisted Val around and toppled her onto the bed. Before she had time to think about it, her tongue was scribbling tiny circles over the pink labia and dipping into the carmine depths of Val's open vagina. She found the slick little nub she searched for and sucked it, her mouth and chin wet with the juices of Val's excitement.

Such a powerful feeling of *rightness* filled her that she felt she would burst if she did not express it in song. Soon Val was bucking up against her tongue, crying out — very close to that elusive soprano, Lillian thought fleetingly — and then Val relaxed in Lillian's arms.

But Lillian couldn't stop. Val pulled her up until her mouth was even with those pale nipples. Lillian's mouth closed on the soft flesh and Val groaned as Lillian's quick tongue and strong lips explored her body, licking, nipping, sucking, feeling the silky softness of a body like her own. Like the one she admired in her mirror every day.

The "singing" lessons continued, and each time was more passionate and uninhibited than the time before. Lillian worried about her future, about how she would ever have the courage to leave the valley, how she would grieve the loss of Val's company... Val's lovemaking... Val's love. Yes, Val had expressed undying love to Lillian and had begun to openly court her. They were seen together often in the small towns and beyond, in exciting places that made Lillian feel like a child at the State Fair. There were so *many* women who loved women — she hadn't known.

And then one day the dreaded phone call came. Lillian clutched her heart as she hung up the phone. Domingo Garza and his wife and the four brothers of Valencia Maria de los Angeles Garza would be pleased if Miss Lillian Barry would come to their home, Bella Vista, on Sunday afternoon for the purpose of an interview.

Lillian decided to leave town immediately.

Or to kill herself.

But either way, she would never see Val again, and that was not acceptable. She was deeply in love with Val Garza and finally decided to submit herself to the inquisition.

Val came for her in the sleek, black, chauffeur-driven Lincoln which bore the big silver *G* on the "continental" trunk. She was dressed in her best black bolero jacket and matching pants, and her boots glinted in the sunshine. Because the driver's ears were so close to them, they sat solemnly on the back seat and spoke little.

They arrived after a slow and dusty ride between what had once been, before the last hurricane, rows of stately palm trees. The white house rambled over at least an acre. Its red-tiled roofs angled toward the blue sky like cardinals on the wing.

Soon Lillian was seated in a straight-backed chair in front of an outsized desk, behind which sat Val's father. The brothers all stood against bookcases along the wall and looked on with interest. Olivia Garza was seated in an elegant cane rocker to her husband's left. Val stood stiffly at Lillian's side.

As Val's father began speaking, Lillian thought she would probably faint and that would be that. Barely aware of the perfunctory greetings, Lillian picked up the thread of what Mr. Garza was saying with, "Do you plan to have children, Miss Barry?"

Lillian answered truthfully, "I love children and have always hoped to have children of my own someday."

Olivia Garza spoke, her clear voice ringing against the tiled floors, "What is your preference in matters of religion?"

My God, Lillian thought, *did they plan to have*

her killed? What was the significance of that question? And why all these questions anyway? Just get on with it. She was ready to defend her love for Val with her dying breath, if that's what it would take. But she answered evenly, "I am a good Catholic," and she crossed herself for extra measure.

She noticed as the brothers' heads all dipped in unison. Her attention then centered on Domingo Garza. He pushed back his chair and crossed his legs at the knee, a delicate soft leather boot peeking from beneath perfectly hemmed trousers. "Let me tell you something, Miss Barry, about my family. We have a very strong belief in our children and wish to see them happy above all else. That is — above all else except the future health of Garza Citrus. I have four sons, and one would expect that at least *one* of them would be interested in growing the grape-fruit..." He glanced at his sons, who all looked straight ahead. "But — they desire other careers. However, my daughter has always been my partner. When she was a baby girl, she would cry to go to the orchards with me... struggled to help me set out the smudge-pots when she was no taller than this." He held his hand out level with the desktop. "She is the one who went to Texas Agriculture and Military school to learn all the modern ways to grow grapefruit — even about cloning trees." He looked at his daughter fondly. "She is the one who will run Garza Citrus."

Lillian felt Val shift slightly.

Domingo Garza then dropped the bomb. "What are your feelings toward Valencia?"

Lillian wanted to look at Val, but she didn't. She lifted her chin and looked directly into Garza's moss-green eyes. Eyes just like those of the woman at her side. "I love her."

"What does that mean, Miss Barry? Does it mean the same feeling that a woman has for a man? That you would love her forever and not leave for any reason except death?" He leaned forward, his brows knitted above his aquiline nose.

Lillian stood, not sure at all where the afternoon was headed. "I have not been asked for a promise of anything like that . . . I mean, Val has not —"

Olivia Garza stood also and held up a delicate hand. "Our daughter wants to *marry* you, Miss Barry, and I have the same concerns about you that I would have about any of my daughters-in-law." She looked coolly at her sons. "That is, if I ever have any."

Lillian sat. The air left her lungs and her knees had no bones. She tried to assimilate it all but stopped trying because her attention seemed to naturally gravitate to a large wedding portrait of Domingo and Olivia Garza. Lillian wondered, as her heart began to pump blood to her extremities again, how she would look in white.

Park and Ride

I wouldn't have been hiding in the cold dark of night in a stranger's backyard if I hadn't made the accidental discovery that Linda and Mary, two other women passengers on my regular downtown bus, were having an affair.

With each other.

I tried taking an earlier bus so I wouldn't have to see what was going on between them. But, *not* seeing gave me a stomachache. I couldn't stand not being part of their illicit excitement.

They didn't know I was alive. At least, I don't

think they did. I found out their names by listening as I sat behind them most mornings and evenings.

It all started one morning in early November. The Dallas weather had just become consistently cool enough to wear a sweater or coat every day. I boarded the 6:50 A.M. Park-and-Ride Charter for downtown, just like I always did. But for some reason, instead of opening the newspaper, I let my gaze wander over the other passengers. Only a few people ever acknowledge each other beyond a nod of greeting. You never break the protocol and insinuate yourself into anyone else's space. But that morning, the two women in front of me caught my eye. They were sitting close, but not speaking much.

There were a handful of riders, mostly women, who were friends from the same suburban neighborhoods, who sat together and chatted about children, church, or families. The rest of us, men and women alike, sat behind sunglasses or stared at newspapers and books — unseeing and unseen — as we were carried into the glassed-in downtown world where we earned our respective livings.

And then, there I was, hiding in an unfamiliar backyard like some jealous wife, with my car parked on a side street. I had walked in the shadows up the alleyway, passed through the sagging back gate, and was surprised to see the lights on in the house and the blinds open at an angle that allowed me to see into the bedroom. My feet were damp and cold from the effects of yesterday's rain and I felt like a criminal hunched up against the wind, peeping in at someone else's happiness. My insides were churning with adrenaline and a kind of excitement I had never known. A burning ache of singular longing filled me, constricting my throat and drying my mouth.

The scene framed within that slat of light was for that moment the center of my world. As Mary came into the room, I ducked down instinctively, though I knew I was hidden by the dark. Her jacket was already off and she tossed it across a chair. She turned, laughing, and reached out to Linda, pulling her through the doorway and into the room. They both faced the window, and for a moment it seemed like they could surely see me. But then they turned away and my heart steadied a bit.

I knew I shouldn't be there, but I couldn't help myself. Lately, it seemed they had almost flaunted their lust in front of me. Flirting, undressing each other with their eyes . . . and touching furtively as they sat together in front of me on the bus each morning and each night.

And so I had finally done it. Followed them from the bus-stop parking lot and crept into the backyard of the house I had found. I had driven back and forth in front of that house like some lovesick teenager, longing for a sight of God-knows-what.

My nerve was leaving me and I was about to turn and escape when Mary sat on the bed. She had changed into a filmy negligee. Linda sat down beside her, brushing Mary's long brown hair. She had also shed her working clothes and was wearing a man's short dressing jacket. Her long bare legs shone in the gentle overhead lights. Suddenly Linda stood up and then crawled on her knees on the bedspread until she was directly behind Mary. Then she sat, her legs straddled out along either side of Mary's hips. She leaned in close and let one long-fingered hand trail down over Mary's breast while she continued to brush her hair.

I watched her fingers move over that breast, saw the nipple grow stiff under her negligee, and felt a thrill run from my vagina down my legs to the backs of both my knees. Watching these two women was making me horny. I began to feel uncomfortable. The cold wind had somehow found its way inside my clothes to kiss the wetness between my legs. I hugged my coat tighter around me and moved closer to the window.

Linda's hand moved the negligee away from Mary's breast, completely exposing it. I could see the blue veins beneath the skin, and the redness at the tip of her dark pink nipple. Linda ran her hand all over Mary's breast, her red-tipped fingers kneading the round globe of flesh, pinching and pulling the nipple until it pointed at me, erect and taut. Just when I thought I couldn't stand it any longer, Linda uncovered the other breast and caressed it the same way.

Mary's head lolled back and I watched her pulse beating in her neck. I could see both of Linda's hands on her lover's breasts. She was kissing Mary's neck, letting her pink tongue flick out and into Mary's ear.

Linda reached around in front of Mary, opened her gown, and pulled it back so that I could see the dark triangle between her legs. When Linda's finger disappeared into that furry place, I felt my body shudder and was conscious that wetness was saturating the crotch of my panties. I moved closer to the window until my breath began to fog the glass. I couldn't get close enough. I wanted to reach out and push her legs apart . . . to see her pink pussy spread out in front of my eyes.

Just as if she had heard my wish, Mary leaned back, spreading her legs so Linda's hands could touch her most private parts. My vagina throbbed as Linda placed two fingers inside of Mary's opening and began to push them in and pull them out rapidly. They glistened with wetness every time they came back into view.

I reached out to wipe the fog from the window and was shocked to see that Mary's eyes were open. She and Linda were both looking directly at the window and laughing. Suddenly Mary was beckoning with one finger. It dawned on me in a stunning, guilty rush that they knew I was there. Had known it all along. I wanted to run but my legs wouldn't work. I was trying to get myself together when the back door flew open.

"It's a *lot* warmer inside . . . Why don't you come in and join us?" Linda was grinning like a boy with a pocketful of crickets.

I swallowed hard and was surprised to find myself walking toward the open door. *I shouldn't do this.* That much was clear, but my groin was throbbing, my panties were wet, and all I could think about was the sight of those fingers sliding in and out of Mary's pink-lipped pussy.

Linda took my coat and scarf and escorted me into the bedroom and offered me a chair, just as if I were an everyday invited guest . . . not some degenerate peeper caught fogging up the window. Mary had covered her nakedness with her negligee. She sat primly on the edge of the bed with her legs crossed at the knees.

"Are you lost, little girl?" she asked, a mischievous gleam in her eye.

"Or are you finally found?" Linda added with a low, husky chuckle.

I could feel my face turn red. I couldn't seem to make any words come out. I just sat there feeling like a fool, albeit a fool with a steamy hot pussy. Linda moved around behind me and patted me on the shoulder reassuringly.

Mary spoke first. "I'm Mary . . . and she's Linda." She pointed a manicured nail at me. "What's *your* name?"

"I forget," I croaked out, smiling like I'd been caught eating cookie dough.

They both laughed and Linda's patting changed to petting. Mary got up, crossed the floor, and knelt in front of me. "You must be cold."

She took my foot in her hand, removing my shoe as she spoke. "Here — let us warm you up a bit."

Soon my shoes and hose were off and Linda was pulling my dress over my head. They tucked me into the bed and then crawled in too, one on either side of me.

Mary spoke close to my ear. "If you want us to stop, just say so." With that she unhooked my bra, and Linda pulled me up so she could remove it.

"Yeah," Linda agreed. "Just say the word and you're free to go back and watch through the window." She raised her eyebrows and intently watched my face for a moment, looking — I supposed — for some indication that I wanted to leave.

She apparently decided that what she saw amounted to no protest, because she leaned into me and brushed my lips with hers. I felt my hips lift off the bed as she trailed her tongue gently down my face and buried her mouth in my neck. Electricity seemed to arc from my lips to my nipples and down to my vagina as Mary's hands roamed over whatever Linda couldn't reach. I felt like I was going to explode with passion and need. I'd been hot before but never like this. It was always a "sometimes" thing with men and slow — not like this feeling of animal need that made me grunt and moan and thrust my hips like they were motorized.

I looked down at my chest and found Linda's mouth sucking one nipple and Mary nipping and licking the other one. One of them had inserted her long fingers into my vagina and the other stroked my clitoris like a concert harpist.

I came with such force that all three of us bounced on the bed. I sighed and moaned my pleasure as each of them in turn rubbed her breasts and nipples past my mouth and all over my face. I had never felt such passion and absolute joy in the act of making love. No wonder they couldn't keep their hands off each other. What a delight.

I came to myself enough to realize that Linda and Mary were kissing each other and clinging together, Linda's legs around Mary, her open pussy grinding against her hip.

I didn't know what to do, but I was willing to try. After what they had done for me, I was agreeable to anything they might ask of me. What they *did* ask was easy enough and made me even hotter than before.

Mary wanted me to watch while she and Linda made love. *Just go in the closet and open it a little so we can see you watching us,* she'd said. The

55

exhibition that followed was the most sensual thing I had ever seen. They fucked each other slow and sweet. Then fast and furious. Linda's whole fist disappeared into the opening between Mary's legs. They writhed and sweated and moaned. I got so hot I began to masturbate. I opened the door wider to get some more air and Mary caught sight of what I was doing. She took one look and her hips bounced faster and faster as Linda held her arm stiff and let Mary fuck her hand.

Then Linda saw what Mary was looking at and extended her other hand toward me. I walked up to her and held my pussy lips open for her and held onto the bedposts for support while her fingers worked in both me and Mary at the same time. I couldn't get in just the right position so I propped one foot on the bed, opening my pussy wider and also giving Mary a full view of Linda's fingers sliding in and out of my gorged sex.

That must have been the last little bit of excitement that Mary needed, because she shoved her quivering groin even harder onto Linda's hand and uttered a long sighing groan. Her body trembled and her knees jerked as her orgasm sent shock waves all the way through Linda and into my pussy as Linda's fingers fluttered inside me. When I came that time, I could feel the juices trickling down my legs. I had never come standing up, and it felt like I was just one big pussy, hanging on Linda's fingers like a limp dishcloth. I slid off her hand and lay down exhausted beside Mary on the bed.

I watched with interest as Linda's wrist, then her hand began to slowly reappear from inside Mary's pussy. Linda twisted her hand gently and slipped her fingers from their wet hiding place.

It occurred to me that Linda was the only one of our trio who hadn't had her sexual needs met yet. I wondered how this would happen.

I didn't wonder for long. I could see that Linda's thighs were wet from her own pussy juices. She lay back on the bed and held herself open and looked at Mary with pleading eyes.

"Eat me, honey," she said in a raspy voice. "Eat me — now."

Mary fell to it with gusto, her tongue stiffened and pink. She jammed it into Linda's twat with gentle force, bouncing her head like a woodpecker. Then she steadied her head and ran her tongue in and out of Linda's pussy, licking her large bulging clitoris, sucking it, burying her face in the wetness.

I tentatively placed my hand on Linda's breast, kneading her erect nipple. She smiled at me and pulled me closer, thrusting her breast into my mouth.

"Oh God, yesss!" she said loudly. "I love it, put your mouth on me. Suck me . . . eat me. I'm gonna die . . .   Unh — unh — unh — unnhhh —"   Linda's orgasm rocked the bed. Her hips pounded the mattress and Mary and I held her down. Finally her jerking movements subsided.

We all straightened ourselves around in the bed, with me in the middle, so our heads were on the pillows and our feet under the covers. We just lay there breathing deeply for a few moments. They both started to giggle at the same time.

Mary said, "Well . . . stranger." She looked at me intently. "Have you remembered your name yet?"

"Yeah," I answered slowly. "But somehow it doesn't seem to fit anymore."

They both looked at me inquiringly.

"It's Prudence."

Celebration

Bobbie closed the lid on her toolbox and pushed her glasses up on her nose. She squinted, trying to see the woman who was standing inside the Lesbian Center library talking to Meg, the librarian. *Well, crap. Another old butch,* Bobbie thought. *Where the hell are all the fluffs these days? They sure ain't here at the workday. You'd think some of them would've signed on to make curtains or some damn thing . . . Oh, well.* She opened her metal toolbox again and selected a red-handled monkey wrench and a can of pipe dope to fix the plumbing leak with. She turned her baseball hat around, pulled it down snug over her short gray hair, and crawled under the sink.

"You use some help?"

The loud voice startled Bobbie and she rapped her ear against the maze of pipes. She looked up through the open drain hole and saw a single dark, unblinking eye looking down at her. *Looks like a shark,* she thought. *Let her in here, she'll probably eat one of my limbs off.*

"Name's Jean," the eye said. "Whatcha doing in there?"

Well, goddamn. Bobbie unwound her long limbs and backed out from under the sink. "I'm fixing a leak." Still crouching, she looked up at Jean — a short muscular woman with a square chin, white hair, and red cheeks — previously identified as the shark-eyed butch. She measured the interloper for signs of competence and seeing none immediately visible, she said crisply, "Just about through. Thanks for the offer, though."

Jean gave a little half-smile and, seeming to study Bobbie for a moment, tucked her chin against her chest. "Nice set of box-ends." She nodded in the general direction of Bobbie's open toolbox.

Bobbie's hand went to the top tray, her fingers resting lightly on the set of shining box-end wrenches. "Thanks . . . belonged to my father."

"Didn't catch your name."

"Uh, sorry. I get to working, I lose my manners. Name's Roberta, but everybody calls me Bobbie." Bobbie made a move toward the open sink cabinet. Never comfortable with chitchat, she had run out of forbearance. The leaky pipes were calling.

"Nice to meetcha. Like I said, my name's Jean.

And I'm pretty handy with a lot of things." She stuck her hand out at Bobbie and, much to Bobbie's chagrin, continued talking. "I just retired and decided to volunteer down here."

Bobbie rose, stretching to her full height of almost five-eleven. Creaky and stiff from crouching under the sink, she grasped Jean's hand and pumped it. "Yeah?" she asked, interested in spite of her characteristic loner's reservations. "I just retired last year myself. What'd you retire from?"

"Marines . . . motor pool. Thirty-five years."

Damn. Must be some tough dyke. All that pressure — all those years. Sensing a need to compete, Bobbie straightened her shoulders. "That's great. You must've joined up about the same time I signed on as dispatcher with the highway patrol." She watched Jean's face for some sign of approval but she didn't find what she was looking for, unless that same little half-smile meant something.

"Yeah — probably did. That'd been around nineteen fifty-nine . . . Well . . ." Jean sketched a little salute at Bobbie. "Guess I'll let you get back to your plumbing. Nice talking to you. Maybe we'll run into each other again around here. I'm signed up for roofing." She turned and left the room, leaving Bobbie standing there bemused.

During the next few days Bobbie was aware of Jean's presence as they each tended to their duties at the Lesbian Center. She could hear the muffled pounding that signified shingles were being applied. Once, when she was getting some tape from her truck, Jean drove into the parking lot and parked her big black Suburban alongside.

They nodded and talked for a moment about the weather, the sorry state of the Center's roof and plumbing, and how the slut-puppies had wallowed out the sofa-springs in the TV room, and then each woman went her separate direction.

That same day, Bobbie had just settled herself for lunch at her favorite table on the shady patio when Jean appeared and spread an olive-drab USMC blanket across the brick path in a patch of sunlight. She sat on it, spread her lunch and, catching Bobbie's eye, said, "Sun feels good on my shoulders. That roofing'll give ya the shingles." She grinned slyly at Bobbie, seemingly pleased with her pun. "Care to join me down here?"

Well, goddamn. Bobbie was at a loss for the proper etiquette. Butches didn't share picnic blankets, did they? She felt a bit pursued, but she shook it off and moved to the end of the table that was closest to Jean's blanket. "My knees won't let me get down there. Crawling around under this old place has got me pretty stove up." She tore off a chunk of sandwich and chewed purposefully as the warm silence grew.

"Aren't we a pair, though?" Jean leaned back and pulled her overall straps off her shoulders. Before Bobbie could politely look away, Jean flipped the tail of her T-shirt up and pulled it off over her head.

Bobbie noticed that Jean's breasts were small and firm. It took her breath away that Jean had been so bold. The outlines of those pert nipples seemed to glow brightly in her mind's eye long after Jean had covered them by holding the shirt loosely against her chest while she munched the sandwich in her other hand.

Bobbie was puzzled for a moment when Jean resumed talking. Jean's last words had been chased out of Bobbie's mind by the surprising display of bare skin.

"I mean," Jean continued, "here we are, working our hearts out for this place, and nobody around to even give us one of those massages they're always advertising." She kneaded her bare shoulder. "I mean, sunlight does a pretty good job on my arthritis, but it'll never take the place of real live body heat."

Bobbie got an immediate image of her hands rubbing Jean's freckled shoulders. She swallowed a bite that hadn't been chewed enough. She felt confused and ashamed of herself for having such thoughts about Jean. It was plumb *queer* — to think of another butch that way. Like two *men* together, for Christ's sake. And — well . . . that was same-sex or *something*.

Sometimes Bobbie had a hard time remembering that she was a woman. It was as if she lived from the neck up, inside of her own head most of the time. As if she really didn't *have* a sex. Not in the "regular world" sense of the word. She thought of herself as *butch*. And her life was carefully contained within a structure of butch/femme rules, all held in place by her strict adherence to them.

She watched as Jean rose and this time turned demurely away from Bobbie before she raised her arms to don her T-shirt. Bobbie's gaze slid down Jean's back just ahead of the descending clothing. Past the dimpled shoulder blades, down into the delicate depression that closed at the base of her spine into an inviting valley.

Jean bent forward to shrug on her overall straps. She turned quickly to face Bobbie. "Gotta hit that roof again. It's almost done." She smiled her peculiar half-smile and cocked her head to one side. "And so am I." She stood for a moment squinting up at the sun and rubbing her shoulder.

Bobbie knew she should probably say something, but the confusion she was feeling and the poorly masticated sandwich rumbling in her stomach combined to keep her mute as Jean put away her lunch things and folded her blanket.

"You're . . . ah — *hurrumphh.*" Bobbie cleared her throat. "Doing a good job on that roof . . . place is beginning to look pretty classy."

Jean made a fist and poked at Bobbie's biceps. "Sure is, isn't it?" She looked around the patio and nodded toward the access door to the basement where Bobbie had been working. "And all the heads flush and there's hot water in the galley."

Bobbie frowned her puzzlement at Jean.

"I mean, the *toilets* work and there's hot water in the *kitchen,* thanks to your capable hands."

Bobbie blushed and felt her ears light up. She jammed her shameless hands out of sight into her Levi pockets. "Uh . . . thanks." Bobbie felt confused but proud. *Damn* proud. They *had* done a good job of repairing the aging building that housed the Lesbian Center. It felt good to share that feeling of accomplishment with someone else. Even if that someone was an unsettling lesbian who dressed and looked butch — but acted like she wore lace underwear.

* * * * *

Grand Re-Opening Dance posters appeared on
every wall and door as "Clean-up/Fix-up" month at
the Lesbian Center drew to a close. Bobbie and Jean
continued to work hard and met daily for lunch on
the patio. Other women — young and old, junk food
and granola, lipstick and leather, butch, femme, and
"bi" — all came, worked, fought, cried, laughed, and
left again without managing more than a peripheral
entry into Bobbie's consciousness.

But Jean was there, in her paint-splattered
overalls and faded lavender T-shirt, working away at
the calluses Bobbie had grown around her much-
wounded heart. Bobbie hadn't *ever* had a friend. Not
someone to work with and talk to and chuckle with
about the Amazon versus baby-butch war taking
place every afternoon on the softball diamond in the
park across from the Center.

She had lately taken to pressing a razor crease
into her starched Levis and making sure the
turned-under cuffs were *just* the correct distance
away from the double-tied laces of her newly
washed, white canvas deck shoes. She got a haircut
that allowed her casually upturned collar to rest just
under the shortest line of silver curls. Her chambray
shirt showed her blue eyes to advantage and she
took to leaving her baseball hat on the truck seat
every day.

Finally, the big night was at hand. Bobbie didn't
usually attend the dances at the Center, but tonight

was different. Jean had called it a celebration for a job well done, and something she wouldn't miss for anything short of a no-cost body transplant.

The large room was filled with noisy dykes eating, hooting, laughing. Some were entwined in darkened corners, early in their passionate pairings and so lost in feeling for each other that to Bobbie they seemed like panting, writhing, alien organisms. She was embarrassed by their display of bold and lusty enjoyment.

The emcee was at the microphone, shushing the crowd. "Quiet, please! Tonight we want to thank some very special women. We wouldn't be here tonight if they hadn't been so unselfish with their time. When I call your name, come up here on stage where we can all see you!"

Bobbie was looking around for Jean and didn't realize her own name had been announced until someone poked her shoulder. She felt her face turn red as she was tugged toward the bandstand. Being noticed was not something she looked forward to. In fact, if she had known what they were up to, she probably wouldn't have come. Not even for Jean. But here she was standing by the emcee, knowing that her red ears were clashing with her best leather and turquoise bolo tie.

"All you women remember to blow a kiss to Bobbie every time you sit on one of those commodes. Weren't for her, you'd have to line up again out back for Jessie's camper potty."

Bobbie blushed anew at the thought of all those bare bottoms and puckered lips. The roar of laughter and applause finally died down and the emcee continued. "And now we can keep all our pots and pans in the kitchen when it rains — instead of under the leaks — because Jean has fixed our roof!"

Jean, dressed in black jeans and a crisp white shirt, stepped from the crowd and bounced up the steps to grab Bobbie's arm and stand close beside her. She whispered in the emcee's ear and, to Bobbie's dismay, the emcee again asked for silence.

"We've had a request and I think it's *very* appropriate. Jean and Bobbie will lead off our first dance."

Another roar went up as the band began to play "Dream Lover" with a fifties beat that grabbed Bobbie in the pit of her stomach. She felt herself being led down the steps and onto the floor. Jean snuggled herself close to Bobbie, resting her head on Bobbie's shoulder.

Holding Jean the only way she knew how, Bobbie started across the floor. She realized with a rush of relief that Jean was letting her lead. She relaxed a little and let her hand slide down toward Jean's waist, seeking that sweet place she had glimpsed on the day of the boob-flash.

Bobbie tucked her chin down against her collarbone and murmured into Jean's ear, "Thanks. I appreciate you being such a good sport about this, letting me lead and all."

Jean leaned back and looked up at Bobbie, that vexing little half-smile playing about her mouth. "It's the only way I know how to dance ... and besides, I'm the short one." She lowered her eyelids and then looked back up at Bobbie. "I'd like to dance like this with you all night, unless you have other plans." She snuggled her head into Bobbie's neck and pushed closer until they were touching from the knees up.

Bobbie felt an almost-forgotten flutter of feeling gather in her groin. She swallowed hard and tightened her hold around Jean's shoulders. "Nope," she finally answered. "Got no other plans."

She stepped out and bent Jean back in an elegant dip, and felt her heartbeat pick up a rhythm that predated the band by at least a million years.

Made to Order

I grabbed the phone and propped it between my
ear and shoulder and continued to rip the electric
scissors through a piece of grape-colored wool while I
answered. "Downtown Tailor Shop. What can I do for
you?"

The line was quiet for a second, then someone
drew a breath and spoke. "I would like to make an
evening appointment for a special fitting."

The woman's voice was low and well-modulated.
A voice accustomed to issuing orders. My stomach
did that funny little rock-and-roll job it always does

when I hear those two words, *special fitting.* I stopped the scissors in mid-snip and held the phone closer to my ear. I didn't recognize her voice, but then I might not. A few of my "special" customers hardly spoke at all.

"Have you been in before?" I asked, trying to connect a face with the voice.

"No ... You were highly recommended by an associate of mine." Her voice dropped on the word *associate* and vibrated with breeding and class. "I have an extremely tight ... schedule. Can you see me some evening this week?"

I riffled the pages of my calendar and decided to forego that evening's tae kwon-do class. From the barely controlled urgency in this gal's voice, I figured a special fitting session with her might do a lot more for me than kicking short guys in bathrobes.

"Yes." I said into the phone. "Coincidentally, I have *this* evening free. Can you be here by seven?"

"No ... I have an after-hours board meeting. Is nine too late?"

The muscles of my lower abdomen gathered in a quick flex as her voice dipped again over *after-hours.* Power shoulders and slim hips and blunt-cut blond hair moved in a montage across my inner eye like models on a runway.

I managed to get a grip on my fantasy long enough to answer, "Nine's fine, but be sure to come to the lobby entrance. I lock the street door at six."

"All right. I'll see you then." The line buzzed in my ear for a second and I realized she'd hung up without leaving her name. Oh, well. Some of them were like that. Secrets and shame and guilt that tied them up into knots that could take me *hours* to undo.

I whistled, my spirits dancing now, thinking about the evening ahead. I hung up the garments I had finished for tomorrow and gave some energy to neatening up the shop. It made me feel good to touch the dress forms and secure the lines on the pressing machine. For so many years it had been my father's business with me as the ever-present apprentice, but it was all mine since his retirement. I closed the case of bobbins and dusted the shiny steel sewing machine, admiring its economy of design as I covered it. I loved the shop's downtown location, on the street level of a building full of lawyers, accountants, and insurance types.

It had always been a trip for me to wait on the powerful and exciting people who came in and out all day. As styles changed and women's business suits looked more and more like those of their male counterparts, their special needs had fallen to me, as the only woman present. Me, the career butch, who loved every woman in sight. What a life. What a goddamn, made-to-order life.

It took me only a few minutes to finish cleaning up and close the shop. I turned the sign in the street-side window and rolled down the heavy steel looter screen, securing the locks where it clanked into place along the floor. Then I locked the massive wooden front door and dropped the iron bars behind it into their rests. Helluva routine — but necessary in my downtown world. I could handle myself pretty good but why take a chance? Life was too fine to miss even a minute laid up in traction.

I unlocked the drop-box which allowed customers to leave off jobs from the lobby side, locked the big brass double doors beside the box, and turned out the "back in half an hour" sign.

Now.

Time for the important stuff. I grabbed a quick sandwich and a beer from the little fridge and watched an hour of bad news just so I could see my favorite weather girl. The knowledge that she was also one of my special customers made it better than dessert.

I hurried into the back room, undressing as I went, and stepped naked into the shower the city made me maintain. I never complained about the cost — it came in handy for a lot more things than washing off accidental chemical spills. I soaped and scrubbed, relishing the thoughts of what my new special customer would be like. She had sounded like a looker.

My excitement grew as I dried my body. You couldn't turn around in the back fitting room without seeing your reflection in at least one full-length mirror, and I could see that my hours in the gym and on the mats kick-boxing had not been wasted. I looked pretty good for thirty-seven. I dried my curly brown hair, flipping a comb through it, making sure my Elvis wave would fall just right when it dried.

I wondered what I should wear. What flavor should I give the evening? Spicy? Latin leather pants with silver-toed boots? Or biker denims with a tight white T-shirt? Since I didn't know my new customer's preferences I decided to go with stone-washed cotton slacks and a crisp white shirt, collar up and open at the neck. No underwear, of course. My bare feet were tanned and looked good in white rubber thongs, but seemed somehow vulnerable, so I changed into soft black boots.

All that remained was to check my stash of toys. I disliked thinking of it as a trick bag. After all, it wasn't like I ever charged *money* for a special session.

Yeah, everything was ready. Each device sealed up in its own little bag, all clean and shiny, at least where it was *supposed* to be shiny, like the chrome studs on the black dildo harness. I did love to wear that one. There was something absolutely transcendent about having a woman on her hands and knees in front of me, her ass up and legs spraddled out — begging for me to do it faster, harder. I had perfected the use of that little rod into an art form. And I loved the way it was made, with those smooth nubs on my end of it, bouncing against my clit every time I shoved it into some power-mama's pussy.

I checked my supply of condoms. I never used my little fuckers on anyone without making sure they were covered tight, slick and safe. Some of these women wanted me to do things to them with my toys that they would have cut a guy off at the knees for even suggesting.

Aroused by these thoughts, I practiced a few tai chi exercises while I waited for my new customer to arrive. I didn't have long to wait before I heard the bell chime.

I peeked before I opened it. A person couldn't be too careful. It *was* a woman, all right. A big, rangy, *tall* woman. I watched her as she pushed the button again, then turned away, presenting her back to the doorway in the old Irish custom of showing goodwill toward the person inside the house. It was a courtesy, to offer oneself unarmed and vulnerable, therefore harmless. God. How I loved women with *customs* and *habits* and *routines.* When they cut loose, they were the wildest.

I opened the door and she turned and stepped into the shop. She had looked big through the peephole, but face to face, she was bigger than I'd imagined. She stuck out a square, long-fingered hand and gripped mine hard. I stood up straight, leaned my weight on the balls of my feet, and tried to make myself seem taller. It was going to take some extra attitude to keep this one in line.

Her gaze was a little off-center, her eyes not quite meeting mine. Shy, I thought, and my butch heart gladdened. She shook her head, tossing her hundred-dollar-a-month blond hair back across her shoulders. Long legs — long strong arms. Damned if she didn't look like Dietrich's character from *Blue Angel* gone golf pro.

I remembered my manners and asked her if she was here for a special fitting.

She looked at me straight on for a split second, her gaze sliding past mine in a hurry to look around my shop. "Yes ... I spoke with you earlier ..." Her voice trailed off when I smiled and took her by the arm, establishing early control.

"Go on back and have a seat" — I gestured toward the fitting room — "while I lock up."

When I entered the room, she was still standing, working her hands together. She dropped them quickly to her sides and faced me squarely, her chin out just a little. "I've never done anything like this before, I —"

I cut her off, wanting to put her at ease. "It's okay. Just sit down and relax while I ask you a few questions."

She sat, then crossed her long legs and pointed killer pumps in my direction. Her silk slacks rode up her calf. She might have a tight schedule but it clearly allowed time for workouts. *Great* legs. My clit jumped as I projected what it would be like to have those legs wrapped around me.

"You say a friend recommended me to you?"

"Yes. Her name is Graciella."

My knees weakened as memories of Graciella ran through me. Graciella's last visit had turned into a whole night of fucking. The woman was insatiable. She came more often than junk mail and she was still hot when, at daybreak, I put her in a cab for home and husband.

"I see," I said. But I didn't. At least not yet. "Did she tell you *everything* about her special appointment with me?" I was trying to get some idea of what this woman wanted.

"Yes, she did . . ." She bent forward, clasping her hands together around her knees, uncomfortable, I supposed, without a conference table between her and the world. "Let's get down to business." Her voice dropped on *business,* causing my clit to jerk again. "I don't have time for intimacy in my life. It's too messy with my associates in the business arena. I have come here for some physical relief. I need sex. That's why I'm here." She looked down at her hands.

Ordinarily that much straightforwardness would take a little of the bloom off an evening, but somehow, coming from this vision in front of me, it only made me hotter. I smiled what I considered to be my most seductive smile as I took her by the hand and led her to my toy chest. "Does anything here catch your fancy?"

Her eyes glittered and she lost whatever hesitancy she might have had. She indicated my own toy of choice with one long, red-tipped finger. Her lips curved into a small O as I took the black harness from its hook and picked up the dildo she had selected. I guided her back to the fitting room and shut the door which separated us from the rest of the shop.

"Why don't you get more comfortable." I pointed to the daybed against the wall with its piles of colorful pillows. "I'll be right back."

I ducked into a fitting cubicle and slipped out of my soft boots and slacks. Excitement pushed my breath out of me as I slapped the cool leather against my bare skin. The harness fit my hips like a wetsuit. I inserted the smooth red rubber dildo into its nest and buckled the leg straps around my upper thighs. I watched my reflection in the mirror and began to get that old invincible feeling. I unbuttoned my shirt but kept it on. My hard nipples poked against the fabric, making little white points. The dildo peeked up between the shirttail panels like a red crocus growing out of my dark pussy. When I shimmied my hips, it vibrated as if it had a life of its own.

I admired it for the space of one more shimmy, then pulled on supple leather pants, arranging the dildo front and center, snug and firm under the zipper placket. I pulled on black biker boots with wide, chrome-ringed ankle straps and stuffed the hems of my pants inside the boots. By God, if this look didn't have her creaming her silk slacks, nothing would.

I stepped out and strode into the room like a storm trooper, looking to catch her by surprise. And it worked. Her chin dropped and her eyes, gray and heavy-lidded, opened full and round. Then she issued a shaky little smile that soon turned into a grin.

"Oh, yes," she said quietly, so low I could barely hear her. "Oh, yessss."

I pulled her up from where she lay on the bed. Evidently, "getting comfortable" meant removing her shoes. She was still fully dressed except for those wicked pumps. Without them she was still a few inches taller than me.

I switched on the stereo and pulled her close as we slow-danced to a steamy beat, hardly moving my feet, but letting her get used to the feeling of my hard crotch against her. It wasn't long before she was draped over me like a serape, rubbing her cunt against me with a rhythm which would shortly lead straight to orgasm, I was sure.

And that was not what I had in mind. At least not yet. I wanted her hot and juicy and pleading. I pulled away and walked her over to the bed. She sat as her knees touched the edge. I straddled her lap, pushing against her abdomen, holding the hardness away from her pussy, just high enough above it so that she couldn't get her clitoris in contact. I opened my shirt and let her look at my breasts. I wanted her to remember I was a woman, that she was wet with desire because a *woman* had made her that way.

Her hands immediately covered both my breasts. She smoothed her fingers around them in circles, rolling my hard nipples against her open palms. She lowered her lips softly to the space where my breasts met and kissed the skin. Her eyes flew open and she drew back and looked at me with an obvious shock of epiphany.

She *liked* it. I was a woman and she *knew* it and it made her *hot*. She took a nipple in her mouth and sucked gently, then licked it, exploring it with her tongue, rubbing it against her face in a rush of discovery. She moaned and locked her long arms behind my neck.

Before I knew it, she had leaned back and pulled me with her. She lay under me, panting, thrusting. I rolled off and tugged her up onto the bed, turning her so we both had room to stretch our legs. She lay beside me, quivering like a captured fox.

"I want you." Her voice was rough and low with need.

"I know." I unbuttoned her blouse, slowly. I wanted to make the moment last. Her bra fastened in front and when I loosened it, her breasts rose in freedom, creamy pink-nippled mounds of exquisitely smooth flesh. I brushed each small light-pink tip with my lips, flicked them with my tongue. Her hips rose as if my tongue had stroked her clitoris. She was so ready for me that I couldn't resist any longer. I tugged open her slacks and she was immediately on her feet. She hooked her thumbs in both waistbands and her panties came off with the silk slacks as if they were one garment.

I breathed in the sudden smell of her passion as she lay back on the bed, opening her long legs for me. She placed the strong fingers of both hands against her pussy and opened it wide. The labial folds were broad, meaty and red and gorged with veins filled with hot blood. Her pale clitoris rose under its hood of pink flesh, gleaming wet and inviting, the smooth runway of its slick shaft extending down into the dark depths of her center.

With some effort I tore myself away and stood up. I placed her hands on my zipper and she got the idea. She unzipped me and the dildo peeked out, red and firm. She dragged the leather pants down over my hips and before I could stop her she had me turned around and sitting on the bed as she pulled off my boots and stripped the pants from me in one smooth pull.

She sat on my legs, facing me, the tip of the dildo just grazing her pussy lips. She shocked me by sliding her fingers past the dildo and into me. She worked them rapidly, taking me completely by surprise.

She said in a rush, "You're so wet. I knew you would be. Oh, God, it feels so good." She scooted closer to the dildo, the tip of it disappearing into her. She leaned forward and her weight pinned me to the bed.

This was *not* what I had planned. My shameless pussy was grabbing her fingers like a suckling calf. Suddenly her breast was in my face and I closed my hungry mouth on it. I could feel her beginning to fuck herself on that red rod attached to my crotch but her hand was still under it. My twat was full of her fingers and my mouth full of her tit and I had totally lost control of this fuck.

She slid forward and rammed the dildo home. She bounced against me, her inner thighs slapping my groin as she came nearer and nearer to orgasm. Her breath came in grunts as she slammed her pussy down over that shiny fucker and just as she collapsed against me, I came like Vesuvius. My jerking cunt grabbed her hand and my insides shuddered clear up to my teeth.

We lay so tightly together I could feel her contractions moving the dildo against me. She moved her fingers deep inside me and my vagina clamped down again and my hips bucked like I had been on the bottom all my life. But as good as I felt, I wasn't going to complain at this point.

She gently pulled her hand free and raised herself off of the dildo. It made a little sucking noise as it came free and bounced against my leg. She snuggled down beside me and whispered in my ear. "Do you think *I* could wear that for a while?"

My traitorous clit danced as the forbidden vision of her above me, pounding me into tomorrow, gave my tongue permission to answer. "Yeah ... maybe. For just a *little* while."

She grinned, her eyes gleaming like she'd won the lottery, when I handed her a fresh condom and unbuckled the harness.

Ah, well. So much for attitude.

The Stand-Up

I arrived late and had to ask a disappointed squatter to move from my fourth row, center-front seat. She scowled at the ticket I held in front of her face but left with the good-natured acceptance of the truly guilty. The voices of excited lesbians buzzed around me as we waited for one of our own to come on stage.

When the auditorium clock showed the correct lesbian-time, widely known to be at *least* half an hour past the advertised time, the houselights dimmed and an expectant shushing rippled through the crowd. Knots of visiting dykes unraveled and none but the most persistent were left standing, preening their needy flamboyance until the very last moment, when Babe Dahl strode toward the proscenium and lifted the microphone from its stand.

She shone in the spotlight, her short, straight hair shimmering as she moved briskly about the stage, bowing and throwing kisses, a slim, taut, perpetually moving bundle of energetic acerbity. The crowd roared in familiar expectation as she stood still and slowly turned her back to us, delivering her signature *shtick* by half-mooning the crowd. A rapid but tantalizing flash of one bare cheek and its red cartoon lip print.

The Babe had come to town for three performances and tonight's was her last before she left for the next stop on her tour. I had come the first night on a dare from my therapist. The second night I was drawn back because the laughter had loosened something inside me that had been walled up since my first lesbian lover had dumped me during a messy divorce six years ago. And I had come back tonight because I simply couldn't stay away.

The woman on the stage seemed to have the power to reach into my heart and pull out all the hidden angst, turning it in the light of her shrewd observations in a way that guaranteed a laugh would bubble up from deep inside me. Tears of laughter wet my face and my sides ached from it.

It was better than sex. Better than food. Better than paid-off credit cards. I hadn't laughed like this since I was a girl. Suddenly the world seemed not so threatening, not so difficult a passage after all.

My therapist would be pleased.

I resolved to go to the local gay and lesbian bookstore the next day and purchase every tape, CD, book, video, and magazine either by or about Babe Dahl. I had become an overnight fanatic. Her Number One Fan.

I wanted the night to go on forever. The bittersweet knowledge that Babe would soon be gone colored her last moments on stage with a light that came not from the dancing spots, but from behind my own eyes.

She seemed to speak only to me, to look often in my direction. The bright lights bathed her muscular, feminine body. Her every move displayed a new and appealing angle. She seemed suddenly vulnerable to me, like someone who needed to be hugged and held safe, away from the measuring scrutiny of a thousand lesbian eyes.

I was the first one to stand as she delivered her parting lines. I clapped and stamped my feet and would have whistled had I known how. After one brief curtain call, she left the darkened stage. The houselights came up and I shuffled into the aisle blinking and thinking about how good I felt . . . and about what I would tell my therapist at my next appointment.

"Can you tell me how you feel about that?" asked Dr. Barbara Cantor, my therapist of six years. "Do you feel this comedienne is now the answer to all your troubles, or could it be that you have merely accessed some long-repressed feelings?"

Merely? What a measly little adverb to describe my recent metamorphosis from depressed pessimist to buoyant optimist. I considered her question.

"I think laughter is healing." I reflected some more about how I really *did* feel about Babe Dahl. "I feel like I've fallen in love. I think about her all the time. I catch myself smiling when I remember her voice and the things she said."

Dr. Cantor raised a perfectly tweezed brow. "Love?" One word. It hung there above her pencil eraser as she noted something in my file.

"Well . . . yes. Love. It feels that way." I tried to remember if I'd ever really been in love. "It's like some expectant craving . . . like I don't really exist unless I'm looking at her or listening to her."

The other brow shot up to join its sister.

I realized how I sounded. As if some new nuttiness had overtaken me. Me — a mostly sane, thirty-year-old, divorced-with-no-kids, depressed lesbian-in-therapy. Good job, almost-new car, health insurance with pockets deep enough even for Dr. Cantor's elegant fingers. I had never before exhibited behavior as irrational as my current need to spend all my savings on airfare so I could follow a lesbian comic around the country like a demented groupie.

Heedless of Dr. Cantor's thinly veiled advice to the contrary, I did indeed attend at least one concert a month for the following year. I heard the material so often I could anticipate by the length of her pauses just which lines Babe would next deliver. When she added new jokes or dropped dated observations from her act, it would jolt me. The impact was like seeing an ex-lover's return address on a letter in the mailbox.

I never failed to laugh. I would feel the chuckle grow and rumble up from my solar plexus. The muscles of my vagina would draw in, my abdomen would thrust up and forward, my ribcage would tighten over my lungs, and great hiccups of air would explode from my mouth as glee claimed me. I craved this feeling that was on par with orgasm.

I began to have fantasies about actually having the courage to wait backstage some night and introduce myself to my heroine. This was some leap from keeping myself carefully hidden in the crowds.

In that dreamy state of wishful fiction I manufactured a scene, complete with stage business and dialogue. I would leave my seat before her act was over, make my way backstage to her dressing room, and let myself in with a key which I had skillfully purchased from a corrupt stage manager.

When Babe opened her door, I would be sitting in her chair in front of the mirror with my back to her. The light bulbs surrounding the mirror would light my face and she would stop in her tracks, stunned by the impact of my physical appearance. Dare I say it? Yes ... by my beauty. The famous Babe Dahl would be struck almost mute by the glory of my face and body.

She would inhale deeply and say, "I might ask where you came from ... but I don't really care ... just so long as you stay for a while."

I would turn slowly and rise, knowing she was

lusting after every curve of my superbly displayed figure.

I would speak, low and sexy. "I come from a dark place. You saved my life and brought me back from the soul-dead. I belong to you now."

Suddenly on her knees before me, she would throw her arms around me and bury her face between my legs, then pull away and look up into my eyes. "If you are truly mine, then I can do with you as I will, can't I?"

Our bodies melted together, our clothes disappeared, and we lay in carnal glory on the couch. She spread my legs and her hands were all over me. Somehow I had known her nipples would be dark with wide aureoles. I kissed them until the soft mounds shrank, leaving her nipples standing erect. She covered me, kissing me with a burning urgency, then slid down my body until her face rested on my pubic mound.

The first cool flash of her tongue found my clitoris as she gently pushed my legs wider apart and her hands spread my labia until I felt cool air wash over the wetness. Then her mouth and cheeks filled the space and she pushed her hands beneath me and raised my lower body to meet her moving tongue.

She nibbled and sucked and moaned her pleasure when I came to orgasm in heaving thrusts against her mouth. Then she rose on her knees and turned her body so that she straddled me, her lips still nibbling my center, her marvelous dark and musky pussy over my face. My fingers caressed the red lip-print tattoo and parted her cheeks, and I boldly slid both my thumbs into her juicy middle and she rode them in quick, determined thrusts, almost wild in her need for release.

And then she would pull slowly away and turn again to face me and say, "Will you kiss me there? Down there?"

The remainder of my fantasy was always the same. Me between her legs, my tongue playing a song of unheard-of intensity and beauty on the instrument of her sex. My mouth would pull from her orgasm after thumping orgasm, and she would draw me up to her, kissing me tenderly and pleading for me to stay with her forever, that she could not live without me.

I realized in my conscious life that my infatuation with Babe Dahl must soon have some other fuel than stopping her video and touching the cold screen, caressing her flickering face while I masturbated.

And it seemed to me, each time I attended a concert, that Babe had grown thinner. I had gleaned from all the lesbo-lit I could find that Babe was a single woman, that she always answered interviewers' questions about her personal life with the same stock "on the road" disclaimer. Her face had become more angular and her observations more biting. She seemed to be experiencing some barely concealed inner turmoil. Her bright eyes wore dark shadows beneath them, and an almost melancholy look had come to be part of her closing act as she gazed sharply out at the audiences, her eyes roving — darting — seeming to search through the glare for something or someone.

* * * * *

87

I held the flyer in my hand. Once again I read the cost of the cruise and my fingers flew over my calculator. If I skipped the next two concerts, I could save enough to go on the all-woman cruise which advertised, among offerings from other stars of the lesbian firmament, that I would be "tit-a-lated by the saucy wit of Babe Dahl" as we island-hopped the Caribbean for six nights and seven days.

It was one of the most difficult things I had ever done, but I disciplined myself to stay at home and prepare for the cruise. I called in a marker from a hairdresser friend and had my hair cut and tinted a sexy auburn red. I walked almost everywhere, saving gasoline money. I ate simply and inexpensively and spent hours at my long-dormant sewing machine, making new outfits calculated to spotlight me as the center of any group of which I might be a part. I was vaguely aware that I was in the throes of classic obsessive behavior, but I simply chose not to stop myself. I felt I would die if I didn't follow my dream and, speaking of which, my dreams had begun to heat up.

As if in compensation for not seeing Babe in person, she appeared nightly to me in all stages of undress. I would wake up wet between my legs and buzz-off vibrator orgasms by the dozens. I could see her face close to mine, feel her hot lips as she kissed me, and I hugged myself in frustrated imitation of her yearned-for embrace.

The big day finally came and I boarded the sleek white ocean liner with hundreds of other excited women. I stowed my luggage in my shared room and stayed to meet my two bunkmates, assuring myself that they were trustworthy members of the lesbian nation and wouldn't be likely to sell my gear to finance an island shopping trip.

I swam, rested, and schemed like a third-time cheerleader hopeful. I fluffed my new hair, checked my clear complexion for any hint of blemish, applied a tiny bit of blue shadow to my eyelids, and pinky-fingered raspberry tint onto my lips. A turnaround look in the full-length mirror told me that I was the absolute blue-eyed clone of Shirley McLaine in *The Apartment*.

Excuse me. The *dyke* clone.

There was no denying my lesbianism. It was properly advertised in the cut of my crushed velvet slacks and in the way my vest barely covered my breasts, under which vest I wore nothing, of course. My slim waist showed the effects of my skimpy eating and I looked as good as I ever had. I was ready to stand up for what I wanted. The next few hours would either transport me to a heaven beyond belief or . . . well. I couldn't even articulate what might be the negative result.

I arrived early and staked out a table at the edge of the dance floor, adjacent to the raised stage where Babe would soon be standing. My heart pounded so hard my hand shook as I lifted a glass to my fruit-colored mouth.

Somehow a crowd had gathered. I was surprised to see that, at some point, three other women had joined my table.

The music stopped, the level of hilarity dropped at least two decibels, and a drumroll announced that the show would soon begin. Moments later Babe Dahl climbed the few steps to the podium with less than her usual energy. I had never been this close to her and my excitement was boundless. Up close she appeared exquisite. A pearl among shells. But she did seem thin to the point of gauntness. My heart yearned to hold her close and comfort her, protect her from whatever sadness had caused such a painful change in the woman who had given me back my soul.

I felt my face warm as Babe turned away and slipped her pants down, just barely flashing the lip print to her wildly appreciative audience. My secret fantasy took my breath away as I saw my thumbs disappearing into her center, my fingers caressing that same lip-marked cheek.

Soon she was well into her opening monologue. She had rearranged a few one-liners and added a new joke which caught me unawares. The laugh started deep down in my belly and rolled out into the air between me and the object of my year-long obsessive desire.

She seemed to lose her place for a moment and turned toward where I sat. She broke routine and her hand flew to her mouth in a gesture of surprise. Her eyes searched the crowd as she stuttered briefly and then went on with her usual well-timed delivery.

I must have laughed too loud. My ears burned in embarrassment and I held myself under tighter control for the remainder of the show. For once I lost track of what she was saying as I imagined how I would approach her when the show ended.

I don't know what I expected. Maybe she would simply move from the stage to the bar and circulate among her adoring fans, but that didn't happen. She disappeared from view like a waiter late for his break. I sat for a few moments, stunned by the stark absence of her sparkling presence.

Though disappointed to the point of tears, I managed to gather myself together and leave the room. I headed for the railing and some outside air, somewhere alone so I could consider my next move. If I *had* one.

What happened next was so unexpected that I reeled inwardly at the pure shock of it. I felt a presence beside me and lost my breath when I realized that Babe Dahl had stepped out of the shadows and joined me where I stood looking at the moonlight as it kissed the ship's wake.

"Would you mind some company?" Her voice, up close and unamplified, was husky and tired. I think I answered but I don't remember speaking. "You know," she said. "After a show, I'm always so aware of being alone."

Well, that could change if I could manage to become coherent and express myself in an orderly, unscary, nonobsessive manner.

"You are very good . . . I love your work." *There. That wasn't hard.*

"Thank you." She looked at me, turning her back to the sea. "I'm glad you said that. My *work*, I mean. It is work. Sometimes damned hard, too."

I smiled and nodded agreement.

"I saw you at the front table tonight. Are you with anyone?" Her dark eyes searched my face.

"No," I heard myself say. I daringly added a line of dialogue from my fantasy: "Not yet, that is."

Babe then magically delivered a variation on the

next line from my fantasy — right on cue. "Would you like to join me in my cabin for a nightcap?"

My real self answered, unaccountably honest. "I don't drink."

"Oh." She smiled. "Neither do I. I meant juice. I always have a glass of juice before I turn in."

Two minutes later, I was sitting across from my idol in her stateroom. The big private cabin could have held six or eight of the economy berths. I felt boxed in by my own stiffness and hoped I could relax enough to pay attention to what Babe was saying. From the timing of her sentences I guessed that she was trying to make me laugh.

Finally she said, "I can see that this material needs some more work." She stood and moved toward me until her knees were touching mine. She placed her hands on her hips and gazed down at me with a look of desperate but comic determination. "Where I come from in Texas . . . back in the fifties we had a drought *so* dry . . . that I had a three-year-old catfish that hadn't learned to swim."

I felt my giggle turn into a full laugh but caught myself because the look on her face was one of surprised amazement. She dropped to her knees in front of me and grabbed both my hands in hers.

"*You're* the woman. You're the one, aren't you?" She looked deep into my eyes. "I know this is crazy, but please hear me out."

I nodded.

"Have you been to any of my concerts? I mean steady — at least once a month for the past year or so?"

I guessed it was time to confess, but I was unsure of how Babe would take my confession of obsessive behavior. To come so close to a dream and then to be denied . . .

"Yes. I did, but —"

"But you didn't come for the last two, did you? You weren't in Denver or Santa Fe, were you?"

"No . . ."

Babe looked at me incredulously. "Do you know how hard I've tried to find you? Do you know how much I've come to depend on that wonderful laugh of yours?" She jumped up and stood in front of the door as if to stop me from escaping. "Wait a minute. Don't be scared."

I had half-risen, but dropped back onto the low sofa. This was not going at all according to my plan. Not *badly*, but certainly not anything like my nightly fantasies.

"I can't eat, can't sleep. Can't seem to get it up for anything much these days. The sound of your laughter is the only thing that makes me feel good. Oh, God. I'm scaring you, aren't I?"

I stood upright, facing her. "No. I'm just trying to comprehend what you're telling me."

Babe stepped forward, closing the distance between us in a rush of words and urgent caresses. Her mouth met mine in a tender, exploring kiss. A fire grew in me and spilled out, running down my legs and arms. I was a lesbian raspberry *flambé*.

The next moment we were on the bed and her mouth was on my breast and my velvet pants were on the floor. She ripped off her clothes in a passionate fury and covered my body with hers.

I knew two things in the next few moments: that I had never been in love before, and that when the one you love loves you back, you have found the only thing that really matters in this life.

The Education of
Mistress Odetta

Chapter One
Prelude

My artist's eyes watched the scene outside as my
train car began to move past the station steps. I
mentally composed groups of dark-clad immigrants,
recording in memory the faces of these people who
had seemed to arrive from Europe in neverending
streams since the steerage rate was cut last year,
1904, to ten dollars.

I saw my own reflection in the window-glass. My
hair and coloring were so like that of the Irish
women. My family's two generations in this country
had not diluted the fair skin and flyaway red hair.

A firm touch on my arm wrested my attention
away from the window. I turned my head with

barely controlled impatience, for I had hoped to sit alone with my thoughts on the trip to Boston. A small woman stood swaying in the aisle, one hand holding tightly to the corner of my high-backed bench and the other clutching a large wicker traveling case.

"May I join you?" She cast her gaze askance at the other passengers, mostly men, and then looked back at me, wordlessly imploring me to save her.

I did. I inclined my head and murmured assent as she and her rectangular basket occupied the better two-thirds of the seat. A distant clanging of alarms sounded as the engine gathered speed. My companion pushed down the basket handle and peered over it.

"You *are* Odetta Vickers, aren't you?" she asked. "My daughter's art instructor?"

I studied her with keener interest. She had a heart-shaped face under masses of brown hair swept up in the latest "Gibson" fashion, with becoming tendrils at her ears and the nape of her neck. Her brown eyes were infused with stars of amber, and her full, pink lips still pursed around her question in the barest swelling of a pout.

Struck by the vision of so much paintable beauty, I may have remained silent longer than ordinary reticence would permit. A sudden glint of light from those luminous eyes and a tiny tightening of the lower lids gave new lease to my tongue.

"Yes — uh . . . I am she . . . but which of my students is your daughter? I don't believe we've met, I mean, oh dear, of course I've met your daughter but I don't know her. I mean I don't know who sh —" Now my tongue had begun I could not seem to curb it.

And then she rescued me, her eyes at full twinkle. "I am Violet Beckwith. Lily's mother."

I nodded my acknowledgment of this disclosure. Visions of Lily Beckwith crowded me. The most talented and precocious of my students, the volatile, seventeen-year-old girl always found a way to skirt my disciplines and with her antics turn my class of otherwise staid young women into shrieking geese. I became aware for the second time in as many minutes that speech was required of me. "Of *course*. Lily. A fine talent. A . . . spirited girl."

"Yes," she answered, her lifted eyebrows punctuating an arch smile. "Sometimes so spirited as to try my very sanity."

I could hardly agree more, but had sufficient wits about me to keep a safe silence this time. I cast about for some appropriate answer but before I could find one, she waved her delicate fingers in the air over the basket lid and said, "Pushing this basket down is such a bother. Do you mind if I move it?"

Not waiting for my answer, she quickly lifted the basket onto her lap and slid toward me, then placed it on the bench by the aisle where she had been sitting and smoothed her skirts with a becoming fastidiousness.

"Now," she said, much closer to my ear. "That's better, isn't it?"

Well.

It was and it was not. If hearing was the objective, then of course it was better, but now there was the warmth and pressure of her slight body against my side. The flurry of light touches and firmer graspings of her fingers on my arm as she talked disconcerted me to the point of physical discomfort.

I could feel my face and neck begin to color.

I knew not so much from auditory comprehension as from the flow of breathy words misting my ear and cheek and neck that she was speaking. As if I sat beside a waterfall with my feet in a pool of trembling pebbles, the force of her personality washed over me, eliciting a response of such inappropriate physicality that I felt near to tears. I had completely lost the thread of what she was saying. Something about the showing of J. S. Sargent's work at the Boston Library. My destination . . . and hers too, it seemed.

I dared not look at her. Alarm buzzed in my brain. I had to gain control of my emotions and somehow extricate myself from this . . . *situation*. But my body betrayed me. All the lonely years receded with the passing landscape. The self-denial, the hard-won physical discipline of knowing and keeping my place as a respected teacher and guardian of young women, all seemed only a feather's weight against the surging power of raw desire which slowly consumed me.

My fingers were laced together tightly across my lower abdomen as if to hold back the feelings. Violet Beckwith placed one small hand over the two of mine, gently pulling my fingers apart until she freed one hand and held it firmly under hers, flat against my upper leg.

Fires of unspeakable heat and promise burned between my hand and hers. She leaned very close to my ear and said, "I maintain a cottage in the city. If you like, we could stop there and refresh ourselves before we take our delight in Mr. Sargent's paintings."

I turned to face her. My breath caught in my throat and thrills gathered in my groin as her hand moved slowly along my upper thigh. She lowered her gaze, resting dark lashes against creamy cheeks, and then suddenly looked up again. The look of hunger in those great, dark-pupilled eyes finished any resistance I might have mounted.

With my heart in my throat, I nodded in silent agreement.

She smiled a brilliant flash of white teeth at me and tilted her head back, to show me, I am sure, how becoming and well-modeled were her neck and shoulders.

And they were.

She was visual perfection. I longed to paint her image on canvas. The working part of my addled brain busily prepared a palette of fleshtones mixed of deep rose lakes, cerulean blues, and creamy Venetian ivory. I could *feel* the stroking of the brushes as the painter in me delineated the delicate hollow of her throat and the unexpected strength of her nose and brow.

To my surprise, the conductor announced our imminent arrival at the Boston station. The hour-long trip had floated away, drowned by the rushing current of pure feeling which coursed over and around me, a watershed of expectant excitement the likes of which I had never experienced.

From somewhere deep within came a weakly protesting voice. *Wrong,* it said. *Women don't respond in such a manner to other women. You have misunderstood her intent. She is only being friendly and is overly elated at the prospect of attending a lively art exhibit with someone who shares her interests.*

I looked down at my lap where Violet Beckwith's hand pressed warmly against my upper thigh. A light shudder enveloped me as she again put her lips close ... this time so close to my ear that they actually touched it. "Don't be frightened," she whispered. "I have experience at this sort of thing." As she turned away, I caught a glimpse of a knowing smile.

So much for her intent.

Somehow I managed to leave the train car with, if not all my senses, then at least all of the items I had carried on board. I followed her through the crowd of travelers and out into the cool air of a Boston autumn morning.

"Ah, there is Max." She raised her arm and waved in the direction of a waiting line of hansom cabs and carriages. A liveried driver clucked to two matched horses and a dark carriage, its brass appointments gleaming in the sun, moved out of line and pulled to the curb where we stood. The handsome driver swung down, agile and quick as a cat, and opened the doors for us.

Violet Beckwith leaned toward him and murmured instructions. He stowed away the large basket and my smaller sketch box, then glanced at me with what I thought to be a rather cheeky smile as he bent at the waist in the merest hint of a bow. Before I could gather my skirts and climb aboard, he grasped me about the waist and propelled me up and into the plush cab. He performed the same service for his mistress, his hands lingering a bit on her lissome waist, I thought with a surprising pang of something akin to displeasure.

"Thank you, Max," she told him as he closed and latched the doors.

"Always a pleasure, Madam," said he, dimpling a roguish smile at us both as he disappeared from view.

The carriage moved swiftly, the horses' hoofbeats barely audible over the pounding of my heart and the blood singing in my ears. It seemed I was about to experience something I had successfully avoided since I was a girl and the first longings for intimate contact with my own kind had bloomed in my mind and heart. A dam had burst somewhere deep inside me. A dam of caution and denial. A stream of steadily building passion flowed freely now and on its crest rode the sound of her voice.

Violet spoke lightly about matters of little consequence. The weather. The trip from Wellesley. The paintings of Mr. John Singer Sargent and his women subjects and how they spoke to her from the canvas. I paid closer attention, as she had broached a subject dear and important to me. I dreamed of someday exhibiting my own work, knowing full well that as a woman, I would be denied access to the men's salon. And I lacked the courage to join the group of renegades in New York or Paris. My upbringing as a gentlewoman worked against me.

When I was a child, my family had been wealthy before my father lost his fortune and fled to California, leaving my mother and my brothers and me in disgrace. As the only daughter, I received an education that prepared me for nothing except to become a rich man's wife.

And to teach.

So teacher I became. This position allowed me some dignity but also held me securely in the class of paid servant, a yoke I wore ungladly.

With a guilty start I became aware of my companion's silence. She sat across from me, her eyes studying me intently, a tiny crease of concern between her finely arched brows. I cleared my throat to speak, but she leaned forward and grasped both my hands in her smaller ones.

"Miss Vickers," she said, her voice low and direct. "Odetta...I may call you that, mayn't I? Have I frightened you? Have I misread your true nature?"

Her eyes danced with the sure knowledge that she had *not* misread me. Or my nature. I struggled to articulate some assurance but, to my dismay, my throat closed painfully and I felt tears on my cheeks.

"Oh," she said. "Oh, my dear Odetta." The look of concern flashed again on her face. She swiftly moved to my side of the coach and nestled herself against me, with one small arm tight across my shoulders and the other hand reassuringly on my arm. "Please don't cry. I am so sorry."

She grasped my chin, turning my face to hers. From the bodice of her blouse, she withdrew a handkerchief and began to dry my tears. The spicy scent of oranges enveloped me. The soft cloth was still warm from its confinement between her breasts and this realization gave such a jolt to my heart that I feared I would faint. My breath came in short bursts and a flaming surge of need gathered between my legs.

She placed her dry cheek against my wet one and whispered into my ear. "I want you. I must be with you. Don't be alarmed. I will be gentle..." She placed her hand over my leaping heart for a tender moment, then moved gracefully back to her seat across from me. Her eyes never left my face.

I thought of many things to say but spoke none of them aloud. A magical silence seemed to pulsate in the air between her eyes and mine. She *looked* at me. Her eyes seemed to touch me as her gaze moved languidly from my face to my neck and down, lingering where my bosom strained against the confining buttons of my traveling jacket. The longer she looked, the more ragged my breathing became.

She looked up, dark eyes again engaging mine, and her mouth curved gently into that certain smile that in so short a time I had come to expect. I felt the impact between my legs — as if those lips had placed a kiss directly upon my sex — as if that pink tongue had trailed itself along my burning flesh. A giddy, electric wetness made its presence known to me in a sudden pulsing of my groin muscles. I tensed my legs and moved sedately to relieve the sweet ache, but Violet Beckwith seemed to know exactly the effect on me of her frankly admiring gaze. She smiled wider, showing a flash of her bright teeth, and lowered the lashes of one eye in a wink of such heady promise that I gasped aloud.

I saw then with satisfaction that *my* presence was having some effect on *her*. Her breasts rose and fell rapidly beneath the fine white cotton of her blouse. Her face sobered and she raised one hand to the hollow of her throat. The tips of two beringed fingers pressed against a pulse there, as if to control the flow of blood beneath her satiny skin.

Fainting had become a real possibility for me. I had never known such complete agitation of my whole person. I had tensed my body against the effect of the rocking coach and began to feel light-headed from the effort.

Violet's voice seemed over-loud when she finally spoke. "We are here, my dear." The coach stilled its rumbling movement as she touched my hands lightly with both of hers. "Max will unlock the cottage and take in our things."

I hoped my trembling legs would not fail me. I shifted on my seat and was disconcerted to discover that my excitement had so dampened my under-garments that I feared for a moment it might be visible on my skirt. But my skirt was dark and my long, belted jacket would drop past my hips when I stood.

If I stood.

My seducer was not without pity. She straightened her skirts and averted her eyes as I struggled to compose myself. Max's shadow passed the window and Violet Beckwith looked back at me just as he opened the doors. "Are you ready?" she asked with a hint of laughter in her voice.

Ready? Oh, God. I felt my readiness in every cell of my body and thought it must be outwardly visible as well. My skin felt hot as the fresh air washed over me. All the damp places on my person became suddenly cool as I took Max's strong arm and stepped out of the coach.

My legs, though still trembling, did not disappoint me. I made my way along a brick walk, noticing briefly the reds and yellows of autumn leaves as we walked toward a small Victorian bungalow which stood in splendid isolation amid a grove of maples. But most of my attention was centered on the slight figure in front of me. I was at least a full six inches taller than her. A tightly belted skirt showed her slim waist to great advantage. The fashions made even more popular by Mr. Gibson's drawings seemed to have been formed especially for her shape. Her hips swayed rhythmically as her surprisingly long stride led me up the steps and inside.

Max and the carriage were no longer in the drive. I could not remember their leaving. Violet Beckwith closed the heavy door, locked it, and turned toward me, gently tapping a large, brass key against the palm of her hand. My stomach did a queer turn and my knees echoed an earlier tremble.

"Would you like a cup of sherry?" She nodded toward a small table set with cups and a sparkling crystal decanter.

I shook my head, still mute, like some ill-prepared schoolgirl called upon to recite. She smiled, a hungry look about her mouth. It seemed she had dropped any pretense that we might be just two female friends enjoying an innocent stop before an afternoon trip to the art exhibit.

"This way", she said, leading me toward the lavatory. "I will be waiting when you have finished freshening up."

I completed the necessary business, surprised again by the wetness of my underclothes, and went out with pounding heart to find my hostess.

Chapter Two
Exhibition

The rooms of Violet Beckwith's "cottage," as she called it, were richly paneled in dark wood, and many paintings graced the walls. They had evidently been chosen by someone whose taste ran to the new impressionist painters. Even the magnitude of my exultant physical excitement could not stay me from stopping in front of a wonderful boating scene by Mr. Renoir. My hungry eyes followed every line, drank in every nuance of light and color.

A sigh of longing and delight escaped my lips as I turned away to find myself the object of a similar study by Violet Beckwith. She held out a hand to me, her dark eyes luminous and appreciative in her beautiful face. "Come. Sit with me for a moment. We have important things to tell each other."

She led me to a loveseat positioned before a stone-mantled fireplace where cheery embers flickered, warming the room. I gratefully sat, relieving my unsteady legs of the burden of standing. I don't know what I expected, but it was not that she would place herself beside me ... so close together on that narrow seat that our legs touched from knee to hip.

"You are a very beautiful woman," she said, again watching me intently as if I might suddenly bolt from the room. "From the first time I saw you in your artist's smock — a soft blue beret capping that magnificent flaming hair — I could not stop thinking of you." She looked down at her hands. "And of how much I wanted to have you for my friend . . ." She raised her eyes to mine. "And for my lover."

The word filled the space between us. It passed from her lips and slid along my neck to gather in the hollow of my throat; a pool of warm, scented feeling was poised to flow between my breasts. My skin felt hot.

My neck and face must have colored to match my hair for she said, "I see you have an understanding of the word . . . and that you are experiencing many feelings just now." She placed her hand on my shoulder and leaned even closer. "And I believe that you welcome my attentions." She hesitated, held my face in both her hands, her gaze boring deep into my soul. "Tell me, Odetta. Tell me you want me to kiss you."

I struggled to speak. *Yes,* my soul shouted. My whole existence yearned for her lips against mine.

I gulped and nodded, but she insisted, "You must say it, my dear."

The voice of something imprisoned since girlhood rose in my chest and bubbled into sound. *Yesyesyesyes.* "Yes. I do. I want to be your friend... and your lover." Oh, how wonderful it felt to put voice to that yearning. To have said it at last. Some weight seemed to fall away from the back of my neck and the need to say it again gathered in my abdomen. "Yes." I felt myself moving toward her. "Please kiss me, I —" She closed my lips with hers. Gently — so gently, dry and smooth and womanly. I was transported by the softness of her mouth as she opened it narrowly and began to move her lips against mine. The soft inside was startlingly smooth and suddenly damp and slick as she pressed harder against me.

She pulled away and looked into my eyes with such unveiled hunger that, had I not been almost swooning from the effect of her kiss, that look alone would have brought me flying into her arms. She rose, again taking my hand, as if to lead me through the steps of this new but not unimagined dance.

As if by magic, we stood beside a four-postered bed, its coverlet of downy, rose satin gleaming in the muted light. Her fingers worked gently at my jacket buttons. Soon it lay on the foot of the bed, then she moved behind me and loosened the placket of my skirt. Her lips grazed my neck as she crooned and whispered words and phrases that took my breath

away. "Beautiful ... mmmmm ... so lovely, my dear."
My skirt slid softly past the silk of my underslip
and pooled about my feet.

I found myself sitting on the bed, looking down
into her dark eyes as she efficiently unbuttoned my
shoes without ever once looking away from my face.

She pulled me gently to my feet and stood
expectantly before me, her hands now at her side.
She raised one brow in questioning eloquence as I
hesitated. "Please undress me," she said, laying
waste to my indecision.

Had I been asked, I would not have believed a
human body such as mine could sustain normal
functions of life and breath under siege of such
sensory excitement. But breathe I did, in ragged
puffs and great heaving sighs, as I began to remove
her clothing. I fumbled at the hooks of her blouse
and had to turn her to the light to discover how
they worked. She smiled in that curious way of hers
but she did not help me. Somehow I managed to
open her blouse and unhook her skirt. She stepped
from its confines around her ankles and sat upon
the bed. She held the corner post and crossed her
legs, lifting one foot toward me for removal of her
slipper. I knelt and tugged it off and then removed
the other. She parted her shapely legs and nodded
downward, indicating the area where her silk
stockings were hooked to her bodice.

My fingers touched the downy smoothness of her
upper thigh and logic left me. My hands moved over
her legs in a rush of tactile glory. My fingers found
the warm silkiness at the bend of her knee, and I

was consumed by the need to place my lips against that same spot.

She buried her hands in my hair and pulled me up toward her face. She leaned back, bringing my body down over hers, opening her legs as she pulled me close. She pressed herself against the length of my body, then wrapped her legs around me, holding me in the welcome prison of an embrace that surpassed any heated imaginings I had ever allowed myself.

We kissed.

We kissed until I grew dizzy from passion. We rolled on the bed, thrashing the coverlets about as our bodies began a rhythmic thrusting. Then she slowly withdrew from me — holding me at arm's length, looking deeply into my eyes.

"Oh, my dear Odetta," she said. "Forgive me. I have quite lost myself in this moment." She smiled, a touch of chagrin at the corner of her mouth. "Have you ever done this before?"

If she meant lay with a woman, the answer was no, and if she meant what it was I hoped with all my existence we were *about* to do, the answer was still no. When I found my voice at last, I merely said, "Only in my most private of dreams." The answering look in her eyes caused my heart to leap. She grasped the hem of my camisole and tugged it upward, freeing my breasts. She gasped audibly and lowered her face between them. She kissed the skin of each one lightly, rubbing her cheek against each hardened nipple as she did so.

She removed my camisole and slip, leaving me

only one remaining undergarment below to cover my hungry nakedness. Then she untied my silk drawers and I lifted my hips to allow her to remove them also. I lay nude and panting under her scrutiny, longing for whatever came next.

She raised herself over me and sat astride my naked lap. It was then I realized with a marvelous rush that she had forgone anything as confining as drawers. The moist heat of her sex settled against mine, sending a shock of delight and desire to every fiber of my yearning body. She leaned forward, allowing her breasts to flow over the top of her bodice. They hung full and dark-nippled above my face. She lowered herself until they touched my mouth, their precious weight caressing my cheeks and eyelids as she moved slowly to and fro above me. She arched her back and moved faster against me, her breath coming in sharp puffs, until she stopped, shaking her head again with that smile of chagrin.

"There is something about you, my dear . . . something dangerous . . . you cause me to lose my head. I want this first time to be momentous for you." And saying that, she slid farther down my body until her mouth found my breast. She placed her hands on both sides of it, stretching the skin back away from the nipple, causing it to stand higher. Then she placed her whole mouth around my nipple, rolling her tongue about it in circles, moving it to and fro, then flicking it . . . much as she had earlier tapped the doorkey against the palm of her hand.

My lower body rose to meet the hand she slid between my legs. Her delicate fingers felt cool against those gorged and heated lips. Her fingers slipped inside me, eased by the wetness of my passion. My body bucked as my hips surged forward, straining for a firmer touch. But after only a few delicate strokes of her fingers against that place where all feeling centered, her mouth left my breast and she slid yet lower until I could feel her kisses on my abdomen.

My imagination had *never* supplied a model for what she did next. Her fingers had deftly parted those lower lips and I felt her mouth upon me there. Her tongue moved against me, searching deeper — then back out, across that nub of muscled flesh that raised itself for touching.

I could not stop the thrusting of my hips. She sucked greedily and flicked her tongue against me, her hands now on my breasts, fingers kneading each nipple. She moaned as my breath came in sharper and sharper gusts. My voice escaped my throat as my body drove hard against her questing mouth. I heard myself cry out and, as I did so, she quickened her tongue, bringing me over that edge of utter delight until I stiffened against her time and again, until I could stand it no more and lay weakly throbbing with release.

She pulled herself away and then quickly covered my mouth with hers. The taste and smell of my own sex was musky and wonderful. Violet's lips were fuller now, and she kissed me hard and deep as I lay in her arms, my sex still throbbing and twitching as she rubbed her thumb across my nipples.

She was rough in her aroused state, urgent with need for the same release she had just given me. I had never touched another woman, but I had given myself relief often enough. Everything in me wanted to please this woman. The thought of kissing her down below, as she had done for me, exploded in my mind like the intoxication of some dark and exotic potion.

I raised myself over her and she trembled, abruptly still. Hesitant, I asked, "Do you not wish me to —?"

"Sometimes it is difficult for me to experience that . . . release, unless I am over you. On top, I mean." She turned her eyes away, the darkness in them almost bruised.

Though it was not how I expected to please her, the image of her above me, rubbing her open sex against mine, was anything but displeasing. I lay down and pulled her toward me. Her slight body was quickly astride mine. This time I allowed my eyes to gather in every detail as her passion mounted. Her legs were still encased in silk stockings and her breasts pushed out over the top of her bodice. She closed her eyes and as she thrust faster and harder against me, my heart hammered in response to her urgency and I began to move with her rhythm. I put my hands between us and opened myself so that our innermost flesh touched. She gasped and moaned in pleasure and I felt the grasping of her muscles against me as she reached that point of wild abandon. She cried out, a long series of *ohs* — and then she fell against me, her rich brown hair in disarray across my face and neck. She lay still and I could feel the pounding of her heart.

"Ohhh", she said once more as she raised herself to look at me. "Oh, Odetta."

And then she kissed me until my breathing came faster once more and her hand found my center and stilled that sweet ache with great skill and dispatch.

Chapter Three
Applause

A few weeks later my heart drummed as I read Violet Beckwith's signature at the bottom of a handwritten invitation. A postscript in her strong, forward-slanting hand requested that I give my answer to the driver now waiting just outside the open doorway to my apartments. I lived above the school where I taught art classes to the Beckwiths' daughter and other young women.

I quickly penned my acceptance of Lloyd and Violet Beckwith's request that I join them and their family and a few close friends for the Yule holidays at their home in the mountains.

I held the envelope close to my face and breathed

in greedy lungfuls of Violet Beckwith's personal scent, a heady mix of crushed blossoms and orange peel. My knees trembled as sudden heat spread down my legs and through my groin at the memory of my nose between her breasts, their downy softness against my cheeks. I have come to believe that the lady *meant* to leave me with my new feeling for oranges. I can't view their shape or experience their spicy aroma without dampening my underclothes. (In point of fact, since our intimate encounter before the art exhibition, I seem to be in a more or less constant state of sensual agitation.)

I looked up and found the roguish Max eyeing me in quizzical amusement. A hot blush flashed up my body. I was sure my face colored a red to match the season. The pulse in my throat leaped at having been observed by the man. The memory of Max helping me into the Beckwiths' coach some few weeks ago deepened my blush.

I rudely shoved the note at him, confounded at my loss of control and aggravated by his bold enjoyment of my confusion. He smiled knowingly and executed a graceful, exaggerated bow as he backed away from my doorway. I pushed the door hard against the sound of his booted feet on the stairs and flew to the window where I could look down on the street from behind the shutters.

He exited the building and leaped nimbly up into the driver's seat of the Beckwiths' large coach. He turned and looked up at the shuttered window I stood behind. Then he lifted the white envelope to his laughing face, touched it to his lips, and waved a quick salute in my direction as the coach drew away.

I buried my burning face in my hands and slid

down as far as possible in my cushioned chair. It is one thing to succumb to forbidden pleasures in another woman's bed . . . but it is quite another to discover that what you had thought secret was common knowledge among the servants.

I experienced agonized remorse for having gotten myself into this highly controversial situation, but as I recalled the excitement of Violet Beckwith's mouth on mine while her bare breasts pressed against my own, the fire rekindled between my legs. The sudden need to touch myself was dizzying. I rose from my chair in agitation and soon found myself in the bedroom. I raised my skirts, hastily removed my drawers and stood where I could see my uncovered nether half reflected in the mirror of the vanity across from my bed.

My breathing quickened at the memory of Violet Beckwith half-naked above me. I trembled with sudden fever at the remembered sound of her throaty voice asking me if I had ever done that before.

I watched my pale fingers disappear into the dark triangle and thrilled to my own touch as they slid smoothly in and out of the wetness there. I unbuttoned the top of my bodice, reached in, and brought both of my breasts into view. I admired the way they appeared, uptilted — thrust up over the edge of my clothing.

I fanned out my stiffened fingers and ran them rapidly across my nipples. A fiery need engulfed me.

The embarrassing encounter with Max and my somehow shameful urgency combined into a peculiar need to touch myself roughly. I needed more than just surface stimulation. I craved something else. My knees weakened and I lay back on my bed, appreciating my own nakedness with a lust I had not suspected I possessed.

My greedy eyes fell on the pleasantly thick shape of the candle on my writing table. I quickly procured a fresh one from the box and with the letter opener trimmed one end to a smooth shape.

In a state of pure agitation, trembling from head to foot, I repositioned myself on the bed and leaned back on the pillows to have a perfect mirrored view of the glistening pinkness between my widespread legs.

The melodious sounds of my young ladies, in the classrooms below practicing their music, filtered to my ears. Their muted laughter and soothing violins seemed far away. I slowly inserted the candle, playing my fingers over my breasts in time to the throaty strains of a gypsy violin.

Faster and faster I moved the candle, watching my mirrored hips thrust to meet its movements. Mesmerized by the shape, color, scent of my woman-self, I came closer and closer to that hungered-for release.

The music quickened, grew louder, the bow drawing from the instrument a wild, breathless abandon ... a joyful, stamping, whirling gypsy dance to which my body eagerly responded. Sending me up — up — and over that imaginary hill into sweet ecstasy. My inner muscles gripped the candle tightly as the waves of pleasure arched and rolled through me. I fell back, watching the candle jerk as the spasms slowed.

I lay breathless, spent. I quite simply *could not move* as my brain registered the fact that my door had not been tightly closed and was, to my increased horror, beginning to slowly open.

Lily Beckwith stepped regally into my room with her violin and bow tucked under one arm. She curled her lips into a wicked smile and clapped her hands together in unmistakable applause. Before I could react, she stepped quickly out and shut the door soundly. But not before I saw the flash of white teeth as her smile widened to tinkling laughter so very reminiscent of her mother's.

Chapter Four
Clothes Make the Man

At last. The longed-for day had come. My bags had been packed for a fortnight. Lowering skies threatened snow and bare trees swayed in the blustery wind. Mounds of fallen leaves lay sodden in the streets and gutters.

My breath steamed the windowpane as I stood impatiently watching for the Beckwith coach. I dared not let my mind recall the details of my intimate encounter with Violet Beckwith. I wanted full control of my faculties when the coach arrived.

I wondered, would that impudent Max be the driver? I hoped not. Such effrontery. Such callous disregard for our difference in class — and such contempt for his employer's reputation.

An urgent tapping startled me away from my post at the windows. Lily Beckwith's muffled voice sounded in the outer hall. I scurried to my door and swiftly pulled it open.

"Mistress Vickers, I am *so* relieved to find you still here. Praise the stars. Now I will get home for Christmas, after all. My plan to travel with the Gifford sisters has come to naught. Their mum has decided the family will holiday in the city."

Her bold gaze and the twinkly merriment in her brown eyes completed my discomfort. *Praise the stars,* indeed. *My* stars seemed *most* unfortunate. Now I would have to share with the lady's daughter that same coach her mother and I had used so delicately. And which girl, by the by, I had been carefully avoiding since my shameful performance with the candle. During teaching sessions, the precocious young scamp had taken to staring at me until my cheeks colored and would then clap her hands in silent mime. I prayed she had not told the other girls. And it made me truly ill to think what could happen if she found out about the ardent nature of my friendship with her mother. What a vexing predicament.

Well. There was no help for the situation. I would have to make the best of it. "Come in, Lily. The coach is due any moment. Are your bags ready?"

"Yes, Miss. I have only two pieces. A small valise of necessities and one empty trunk to bring back filled with holiday bounty. And a box of gifts for the family and servants, of course."

My ears stung at the word *servants.* I am sure

she considered me one. An extended trip by coach, enduring the "company" of this pretentious young woman, was the last thing I wanted.

A thumping of heavy feet sounded in the stairwell and to my great surprise, Lily turned and threw herself into the arms of the driver I was so loath to see. He smiled brilliantly, lifted her easily, and swung her around and back to the floor again. She wound her arms tightly about his neck, pulled his face to hers, and kissed him soundly on the mouth.

"Oh, Max," she cooed. "I am *soo-oo* pleased you will be traveling with us."

My stomach lurched strangely at their display of bold familiarity. I caught a deep breath and looked at the two faces now turned expectantly toward me.

I averted my eyes, temporarily choosing the easy way out by simply ignoring the impropriety of the previous moment. My racing blood betrayed me, though, and my flaming cheeks did not go unnoticed.

After much foot-shuffling from Max and poorly suppressed merriment from Lily, our luggage was secured atop the coach and we were finally off for the uplands.

In time I would look back on this holiday adventure as the true beginning of the new, enlightened Odetta.

I had planned to read and reflect on the countryside during the two-day journey from Wellesley to the Beckwiths' home in the mountains, but I had also planned to be alone. Lily Beckwith had changed all that, as the unthinking young so often do. Her mercurial behavior unnerved me to the point of distraction. I would just begin to relax, and then I would become aware of her twinkling eyes studying me intently. My discomfort seemed an endless source of amusement for her. I could not prevent my cheeks from reddening. I feared I might further embarrass myself by swooning into oblivion.

I do not know what I found to talk about. Memory fails me now. Not one conversation comes to mind. Ah, but that night at the inn in the village of Clearford comes back to me in vivid detail. Beginning with Lily's surprising behavior at the evening meal.

A buxom serving girl brought us steaming platters of delicious pork and mutton pie, which was a welcome change from the cold bread and boiled eggs we had eaten at midday. She seemed a pleasant girl, though a bit coarse in appearance, but Lily took an instant and hearty dislike to her and upbraided her for this and that imagined lack of speed or courtesy. I felt quite sorry for her but it was not my place to interfere. From the moment the coach arrived, when the serving girl had greeted Max with squeals of delight, Lily had marked the poor creature as a target for her devilment. I must confess, I was rather relieved to no longer be the object of Lily's attentions.

We had come down to dinner and were just settled at our table when I caught sight of Max in the doorway to the kitchens with his arm around the serving girl's waist. I thought him unaware of his role in the drama until he turned and flashed a killing smile at Lily. If smoke had curled from her pretty ears I would not have been in the least surprised. She paled and trembled like a young mare on derby day.

"I am very tired," Lily said. "Please excuse me."

I barely understood her, so furiously pressed together were her lips. She left the table with cold determination and marched out of the room and up the stairs.

Though he did not appear to see Lily leave, I knew by the sudden tension of his back and shoulders that Max knew exactly what had transpired behind him. I finished my meal in welcome solitude and without further incident retired to my bed.

Propriety decreed adjoining rooms for me and my young charge. And, in truth, that is what she was. Even though we traveled to *her* home in *her* coach, I was yet in her mother's employ, in a manner of speaking, although I was an invited guest. However complicated the delicate shadings of responsibility were, events had conspired to make me uneasy about the possible outcome of Lily's reaction to our driver's lack of fealty to her.

Later that night, tired but troubled and unable to sleep, I discerned the sound of voices in Lily's room. I climbed from my bed in the dark and put my ear to the door between our rooms. I pressed closer, hoping to comprehend the sounds of low conversation, and leaned back in shock as the door moved silently inward, opening to a narrow but unobstructed view of Lily's bed a few feet away.

I know I should have closed the door. But I could no more tear my eyes from the scene before me than I could have resisted Violet Beckwith's attentions some weeks before.

Max stood smiling by the bed with his hands at his side as Lily unbuttoned his waistcoat. Her lovely young body shone pinkly in the lamplight. She was completely unclothed and her loosened hair tumbled in sculptured waves over her shoulders and down her back.

I desired to speak, in truth I should have, but what I saw next froze my tongue. It was too late. I must discover what would come next.

Lily opened Max's loosened waistcoat and he shrugged it to the floor. He raised his arms and she pulled his shirt up and tossed it across the bed. He stood, hands on slender hips, daring her with his handsome smile to complete the task and remove his singlet. If they had not been so engrossed in their own activity, I am sure they would have heard my sudden intake of breath as Lily placed her hands under the thin fabric and moved them in slow circles against his chest. Max tensed and threw his head back in obvious delight as Lily raised the hem of the garment and placed her mouth on one, then on the other nipple of what were unmistakably *breasts!* Indeed. Yes. High and small, but breasts, to be sure. The nipples stood hard and brown and erect.

Pleasant thrills of discovery coursed through my body as Lily helped Max remove his britches. He modestly turned away from her and, in so doing, exposed to me his well-muscled legs. He straightened and I saw, to my utter bewilderment, not a man at all but — what? A man with no outwardly visible evidence of manhood? No. Not that. His body was too much like my own to be that of a man. The full and heady realization of what my eyes were seeing struck me and I almost laughed aloud.

Oh ho! My lovely, haughty, teasing Lily. Like mother like daughter, I see. My merriment quickly

subsided as Max took the younger woman in his ...
her arms. I felt those caresses on my own body, as
surely as if those strong hands held *me* rather than
Violet Beckwith's daughter. Max toppled backward
onto the bed and Lily stretched her body atop Max's
nakedness like a cat on a winter hearth. Then she
suddenly disengaged from Max's encircling arms and
sat up.

"You know, Maxine, you great tease. You know
what I must see."

Lily clasped her hands and gazed at her
handsome friend with pleading eyes. Max languidly
placed her hands behind her head. She opened her
legs slightly and Lily uttered a small cry of joy and
lowered her face to that dark mound where they
parted.

*Oh, yes, my dear. How very like your mother you
are.*

What I saw when Lily raised her head was very
nearly my undoing. My knees weakened and I
leaned heavily against the doorway. My heart
thundered in my ears.

From that wetly gleaming crevice between Max's
legs rose a pink hood of flesh, and from beneath it a
glistening protuberance much the size and shape of
a very large pearl. Shocks of pleasure quickened and
pinched between my own legs and I was aware of
the sudden moistening of my drawers.

Lily's swift reaction to that amazing sight was, I
am sure, not unlike what I would have done under
similar circumstances. In truth, my hand had found
its way inside my nightdress and I was unable to
resist the overwhelming need to find swift relief for
the ache in my groin.

I watched, mesmerized, as Lily raised herself above Max as one mounts a horse and snugly sat, astride that marvelous "little man in the boat," as she called it. Lily synchronized the movements of her hips with Max's slow upward thrusts. She sat back with her hands behind her, grasping Max's knees. Her breasts thrust out as her head fell back in ecstasy. Max's lowered eyes intently observed that area of activity which held my own rapt attention. With each downward pull of Max's hips, the "little man" appeared from the pink depths of Lily's widespread legs and repenetrated those glistening folds with each upthrust.

The lamplight modeled the suddenly taut muscles in her stomach as Lily arched her body slowly, then gasped and crumpled forward, covering Max with her quivering, jerking body. Max's thrusting quickened and she bit hard on her hand, I am sure to muffle her own joy, and then she too bowed sharply upward as her pleasure peaked.

Those moments were more than I could bear. I closed the door gently and crawled beneath the coverlet, furiously bringing myself to that same ecstatic plane.

I lay in the sweet afterglow thinking how quickly the balance of power can change. It pleased me to have discovered my own truth in that old saw. The fruit falls close to the tree, indeed. What other wonders might this holiday bring forth?

Chapter Five
Joyous Noise

It had begun to snow just before we arrived at
The Maples, the Beckwiths' country manor. The
countryside was glorious in its cloak of white. The
last half of our trip had been as much a pleasure
for me as the first half had been miserable. Lily had
sat in red-cheeked silence, pointedly ignoring my
presence, after my comment that she seemed
strangely refreshed from her nocturnal "boat ride."

As we approached, we could see that the huge
house was profusely decorated with garlands of
evergreen and holly across every porch. A single
great spruce on the lawns was dressed in brightly
colored flags and decorations. Max handed the reins

of the stamping horses to a servant and unloaded our luggage.

I confess to some trepidation and confusion at my upcoming introduction to Violet's husband, Lloyd Beckwith. I had not the faintest idea of how to behave toward a man whose wife had seduced me. In truth, it had been more the fulfillment of a lifelong dream, rather than the seduction of an innocent, but no matter the shadings of it, I had still to meet the father of my lover's children.

I quaked at the prospect.

My heart leaped as I saw Violet flying down the steps to greet us. She was even more beautiful than I remembered. As a proper mother, she first hugged her daughter soundly, but very improperly winked at me over Lily's shoulder as she pressed her close. I do not know why her wink should have such a profound physical effect on me, but it did. That same giddy electric wetness between my legs made itself known in a rush.

As Lily was pulled away by the grasping hands and shouts of her three younger sisters, Violet held me close in a warm embrace. Into my ear she whispered, "My darling Odetta. I have missed you. I can think of nothing but you." She held me out at arm's length and said aloud, "How good it is to see you, Miss Vickers. Come and meet the rest of my chicks."

And one old rooster, I thought uncharitably as she led me toward the house.

Though the air was crisp and cold, it had little effect on me. Such proximity to Violet had lit in me fires of breathless longing. I followed her inside and was struck at once by the opulence of her home.

Lloyd Beckwith must be a baron of industry, I mused, a man to be reckoned with on many levels.

She introduced me to each of Lily's younger siblings. Dahlia was twelve, Rose eleven, and the youngest, Aster, was eight. I tried not to think of bouquets. The girls were lovely smaller versions of Violet and Lily, except that they all had eyes as blue as cornflowers . . . well, perhaps thoughts of bouquets were inevitable after all. I wondered where their father was. I could feel myself growing more nervous by the moment.

As if she had read my mind, Violet said, "My husband is away in the village, tending to some last-minute details for tonight's party. You'll meet him later this evening."

She took my hand, holding it firmly in both of hers. "You must be tired from your trip. Come. I'll show you to your rooms."

I followed her up the steps of a graceful, winding staircase to a balustraded landing from which the whole of the great room below was visible, and then down a gleaming hall with paintings hung so close together their frames almost touched. She opened one half of a double doorway and motioned for me to enter. As I did so, she quickly closed the door behind us and my heart lurched as I heard the click of the lock.

She pushed me roughly against the wall, her mouth on my neck, my cheeks, my throat. Her hands beneath my traveling coat held me tightly at the waist as she pressed her body to mine. Her wildly passionate advances left me weak with longing and desire.

She raised her chin and looked deep into my

eyes. "My darling, I thought this moment would *never* come. I am consumed by memories of our afternoon in the city." She dropped her head and nestled it against my shoulder, where my pounding pulse must have sounded like thunder in her ear. So low she murmured then that I scarcely understood her.

But I did. I comprehended with a heart filled by equal parts of wild elation and great trepidation that she had said "I love you."

She turned her face back to mine and kissed me. Her lips parted and her tongue met mine with such energetic hunger that my blood sang in my ears. Then she pulled away abruptly, her breath coming in ragged gasps. "Later . . . tonight . . . I will come to you." She breathed deeply and stepped toward the door, looking back over her shoulder, her mouth curving into a shaky smile. "But now, I must go and play the hostess."

I stood with my arms wrapped around myself, suddenly chilled by her absence. I nodded, my throat closing and my eyes threatening tears. "Yes. Tonight," I managed to whisper, and then she was gone.

I looked around my suite of rooms and was surprised to see that my bags were already by the bed. Whatever else Violet Beckwith was or did, she certainly ran a well-managed household.

I wound the key of my traveling alarm clock and set it for two hours hence, undressed, donned my warmest flannel nightgown, and climbed between the coverlets. I expected to nap and awake refreshed for the party, but I was so agitated by our passionate — and all too brief — encounter that I lay awake, my tired eyes watching the light in the room change as the day darkened and evening neared.

Finally I arose and pulled on my robe just in time to admit a pretty chambermaid. She drew a steaming bath and placed plump towels on a table beside the claw-footed tub. "Dinner is served at six and the party begins at eight," she said tersely as she let herself out. I soaked in the tub, luxuriating in the unaccustomed opulence of my surroundings while I considered the evening ahead.

I was not disappointed by dinner, which turned out to be a thunderous, joyous occasion dominated by the rollicking presence of Lloyd Beckwith, to whom I was presented as "Mistress Vickers, Lily's teacher and my wonderful new friend."

He was not at all what I expected. He was slight of build and only marginally taller than Violet, which served to make me feel like the only tree in a landscape of saplings. He was a consummate fop in his affected manner of attire, from his profuse golden curls down to his small, highly polished boots. And he had the most sparkling wit I had ever encountered. His stories came one on the heels of another as he favored each of his adoring daughters in turn, as well as his attentive wife and even me from time to time.

Throughout the meal, my heart divided its time between my throat and somewhere below the pit of my stomach as I watched the interactions of this loving family. To save me, I cannot remember what was on my plate.

Violet sat across the round table from me and gave me to understand, by adoring looks and brief knowing smiles and even a wink once when all other eyes were on her husband, that she meant to fulfill her earlier promise. I do not believe I have ever been in such a sorry state of agitated emotions.

Dinner was over none too soon and I escaped to my rooms. I stood for many minutes with my burning temples against the cold windowpane, trying to calm my racing heart and cool my heated blood. As I dressed for the party, I caught sight of my reflection in the large oval mirror beside the dressing table. It pleased me to see that the dress had been worth every penny.

I had chosen to wear a gown of dark green satin which showed my red hair and fair complexion to the greatest advantage. It was fitted tight in the waist and had a high, close-fitting collar that buttoned down the side of my neck and diagonally across my bosom. Aside from its cost, which was far beyond my means, the only thing daring about this dress was the sheer lace inset in the front that covered my chest down to the top of my bosom and allowed the form of my breasts to be seen through the filmy fabric. I wanted Violet to notice me. In truth, I wished her to notice nothing and no one but me, and I hoped the gown would help bring that wish to fruition.

My color was high and my eyes were flashing. Anticipation was evidently good for me. I turned, admiring the liquid flow of the skirt as it swirled about my legs. The fitted waist and back outlined my figure in a fashionable yet slightly suggestive manner which suited my present needs exactly. If my head and shoulders must rise above my hosts, at least they could do so in pride.

I made myself wait until I heard sounds of music and merriment before I ventured down the stairs. I stood on the landing surveying the room below. Men and women in holiday attire filled the room; their animated voices rose like the hum of a great engine. My gaze immediately settled on Violet's figure. Her red gown glowed like a Christmas candle and her tinkling laugh floated up to me as she tossed her head in jollity. I stood spellbound, admiring her beauty, until I was rattled by a raucous calling of my name.

"Miss Vickers!" The loud shout caused a brief startled silence in the room and all heads turned to watch Lloyd Beckwith bound up the steps to take my arm and lead me down. I felt my ears begin to burn and was thankful they were covered by my hair. He introduced me to everyone in the room, tugging me from one group to the next. Always it was, "We are so glad to be visited by my wife's artist friend from the city, the *glamorous* and talented Miss Odetta Vickers."

Never once did he indicate I was a paid employee or treat me in any way as different from his other guests. I was grateful, but also puzzled at his expansive acceptance of me. I wondered what, if anything, he knew of his wife's true nature, and how his manner might change if he found out.

I danced and conversed gaily with a neverending stream of handsome men and had entirely too many cups of the heady punch. My eyes always sought out Violet's, and found them watching me, often as not. I felt attractive, desirable, and on fire with a consuming need to hold my lover in my arms and to feel her naked body over mine. My secret burned between my legs in a sweet ache of steamy longing.

The room stilled at the insistence of a clanging gong held aloft by Lloyd Beckwith. He stood on a piano bench and gestured toward his wife, the lovely object of my damp desire, who stood regally before the gleaming grand piano. She had slipped away to change and was now dressed in a close-fitting gown of daring black with a deep and inviting décolletage. A black feather boa trailed from one hand across her bare shoulders and down her back. Her eyes found mine as her husband began to play the lilting prelude of a popular holiday song.

She sang in a clear and powerful soprano, her breasts rising and falling, the muscles in her neck moving exquisitely as she leaned her head back and gestured with her arms. She looked at no one but me and I wondered if anyone else noticed it. If they did, I did not see it. I was enthralled by Violet's beauty and by the force of her gaze as her lovely voice played down my spine and caused a sensation in the roof of my mouth like the taste of maple syrup mixed with snow.

When she finished singing and applause filled the room, I was brimming with such a wealth of emotions that I was barely aware of my surroundings. The orchestra began again and I was whirled away by yet another young gallant, who danced me into the hallway and bowed himself away, leaving me standing before Violet.

She took my arm and led me toward the kitchens, speaking close to my ear. "We won't be missed for a few moments. Come . . . I must have you all to myself for a while." She said nothing more as a servant held out fur cloaks for our shoulders. We tugged the cloaks tight about us and stepped out onto the snowy lawns.

The redoubtable Maxine held the reins of four dappled Percherons who stood under ornate traces, stamping and breathing steam. They were harnessed to a large Bavarian sleigh. The picture they made in the moonlight set my artist's soul to soaring. I looked back at the house with its windows casting long shafts of golden light across the snow and felt the scene settle in my heart. Tears of happiness welled in my eyes.

Max climbed into the enclosed driver's box and clucked softly to the horses. We moved away into the night. Violet grasped my arm as we settled under the cloaking warmth of great fur robes. The sleigh runners whispered across the snowy ground.

"It is beautiful, is it not?" she asked, turning my face to hers. "But not as beautiful as you, my love." We had barely left the drive when Violet embraced me, holding me so tightly that I feared for the seams of my dress. She covered my face with kisses and her fingers worked gently but insistently at my buttons.

I was vaguely aware of the presence of Max and the horses, but my heart and soul and body responded in uninhibited delight as Violet opened my dress and ran her fingers over my breasts. She buried her face against me, crooning and murmuring endearments. And then she stilled, as if by great effort, and pulled away, resting her head against the plump upholstery of the curved back of the sleigh. She found my hand under the robes and held it tightly.

"You are so much more than I reckoned on," she said softly. "I am behaving like a wanton child." She turned her face toward mine, her eyes sparkling in the cold moonlight. "Thoughts of you crowd all else from my mind and my eyes want only to look at you. I have been searching for you all of my life."

The impact of her words served to break away any lingering hesitance in me. I moved decisively, aggressive in a way that was unfamiliar but that I knew was somehow exactly proper for the moment. I took her in my arms, covering her face and neck with kisses, sliding farther under the robes as I raised her skirts. My fingers quickly found the warmth between her legs.

She protested but I could not stop myself. My emotions had been held too long in check. I spread her legs with gentle but insistent pressure and raised my lips to her mouth. A shock of welcome discovery consumed me when I realized she wore no undergarments. As my fingers reveled in the soft wetness of her need, I felt her shudder. Her kiss began to meet the urgency of mine. I covered her slight body with my larger one and held her fiercely, as if to claim her for my own, the hero in me possessing her almost as a prize of battle.

I moved quickly and positioned myself between her knees, lowering my face to her lap, kissing any flesh I could uncover along the way. She had stiffened against me and stilled as my kisses found their target. I felt her fingers grip my shoulders but I could not stop. I opened her legs and placed my lips firmly against her heated center. My tongue seemed to have a life of its own as I wrapped my arms around her hips and pulled her lower on the seat. She gasped as I thrust my strong tongue into her and moved it slowly out again.

She sank beneath the robes with me and began to move with the rhythm of my searching tongue. At first I could barely discern her movements from the motion of the sleigh, and then she seemed to come alive, as if some internal dam had broken. She tightened her knees about my head and buried her fingers in my hair.

I became wild in my need to feel her throbbing release against my mouth. I thrust my tongue in and out, out and in, then settled against her, flicking the stiffened tip of my tongue exactly upon that swelling pearl where release lay hidden. She bucked herself against me and I was set afire by the tattoo of her heels drumming against my back. I fluttered my tongue with renewed fury and was rewarded by a sudden thumping tightening of her legs around my head. She locked her feet behind my neck and thrashed against my face, crying out in sharp, breathy, animal-like sounds.

She stiffened and leaped each time my tongue moved against her. Such power! I lost myself in the wonder of it until her grip on me relaxed and I could breathe freely again. She pulled herself upright in the seat, tugging at me as she went. We both emerged from under the robes into the crisp night air.

My face steamed as if I had just stepped from my bath. She laughed gently and watched me with adoring, tear-filled eyes as I tried to dry my cheeks and chin and pin up my hair at the same time. She pulled me to her and held me close. My heart still beat thunderously from the effects of my wild abandon and from the excitement of having brought fulfillment to Violet.

She turned to me and kissed me tenderly for a long moment, then pulled away. "Well," she said softly, then repeated, "Well . . . my darling Odetta. You are every bit as dangerous as I feared." She raised her voice, thumping her hand against the driver's box, and said, "Max. Take us home now." To me she whispered, "Later tonight we will finish what you have started. I will come to you when the house sleeps."

Chapter Six
The Christmas Gift

I had no wish to return to the party. In truth,
even had I wanted to, my disheveled condition would
have prevented it. I escaped into the silence of my
rooms, drew a bath, and undressed, musing over my
situation. What sort of future might I have as the
occasional lover of an apparently happily married
mother of four lively daughters? My feeling for Violet
had grown from a consuming sexual hunger into a
craven need of such intensity and proportions that it
frightened me. So tense was I with worry and
expectant hunger that my body hummed like
telegraph wires in a windstorm. I do not know how
sleep finally claimed me, but it did.

I woke to the feel of cool, bare flesh against me as Violet settled her body next to mine in the bed. My sleepiness fell away in a rush as she moved her hands under my nightdress, slowly caressing my breasts. She kissed me tenderly, her lips dry and soft and teasing on my face and neck. A surging need for release raced through my veins, converging between my legs with a fury. I was weak with it. Nearly swooning from need, I grasped her shoulders and shook her.

"Oh, Violet. Please — please touch me. I have no shame. I can bear it no longer. If you do not touch me there I will die from longing."

In the moonlight from the window I could see Violet's mouth turn up into that curious half-smile. "Where?" she asked softly, teasing. "Where must I touch you, darling?"

She placed her hand lightly on my lower abdomen. "Here?" She raised herself on one elbow and then covered my burning body with her cooler one, straddling my upper thighs and sitting up as she did so. I was mad with desire and needed more than her sex rubbing against mine. With a burst of energy born of desperation, I turned her easily onto her back, stripping my nightgown from me in one motion. I spread her legs and buried my face in the furry warmth of her center.

"Here," I said roughly, stroking my tongue deep into her. "Here, you vixen. I need you to touch me *here*." As I said this last, I grasped my breast and rubbed it between her legs, pushing my hardened nipple against her sensitive sex.

She leaped from the bed like a woman possessed and stalked about the room naked, hugging herself, looking at me with widened eyes. I quaked at what my boldness had wrought. I wanted to cry, but my stubborn temper bubbled just under the surface, fueled by an insistent throbbing between my legs.

She turned away and stood looking out the window for a moment, her form tense and still, like a Donatello sculpture in the moonlight. Then her shoulders relaxed and her arms fell to her sides as she turned and slowly walked toward the bed where I sat atremble.

She nestled beside me. "I am sorry, Odetta. Sometimes you frighten me a little. No . . . that is not exactly true. My *reaction* to you is what frightens me. I have never before experienced feelings like these I have for you. I have come to want you in my life more than anyone or anything else. Time not spent in your company is meaningless."

My heart lurched as I comprehended the seriousness of her words. I felt the same way. My God. What would happen to us? What could we do?

She pushed me gently back on the bed, kissing me with lips wet and salty from her tears. Passion drove vexation from my soul as her fingers worked magic between my legs. She had stroked me not more than a dozen times when a spasm of release streaked down my legs and up my spine, causing me to jerk and leap under her touch. I trembled and spasmed again and again as she lowered her face to my center and trilled her talented soprano's tongue across that quivering nub where all sensation had gathered.

She held me tight, sucking, licking, drawing from me with her mobile lips all the pent-up need, all the tense longing . . . until I lay limp and sated in her embrace. We fell asleep in each other's arms. Some time before dawn she must have slipped away, for I woke to sun streaming through the window, coloring her empty pillow with rosy shadows.

I rose on this day before Christmas and bathed, fixed my hair and dressed without once being conscious of my actions. I found myself by the door, hand on the knob, and caught sight of my form in the long oval mirror. *Oh my,* I thought, and I smiled at my reflection. *I look like a woman in love.* I tried to arrange my features into the visage I presented to my classes, a prim and proper schoolmistress. But I knew now that a bold and wanton creature lurked just beneath this practiced surface, and she threatened the very underpinnings of my life. I told myself that I must keep her in check. With that admonition in mind, I descended the stairs and entered the dining room where a loud and boisterous breakfast was already in progress.

Lloyd Beckwith leaped to his feet and strode across the polished floor to take my arm and escort me to the table. An empty place was set beside Violet. She looked at me with large, brown eyes that brimmed with dangerous truth. I acknowledged her and the others at the table as my chair was pushed in gently behind me. I sat, lowered my eyes, and gave concentrated attention to the act of chewing and swallowing. Though for the second time in as many days, I could not have recalled what the meal consisted of.

The girls were excited. They laughed and shouted among themselves until Violet looked meaningfully at her husband, who stood in diminutive but effective seriousness and threatened no visit from St. Nicholas unless order was restored. I noted that a look of much feeling was exchanged between Lily and Max when Max brought up boxes of Christmas decorations from below-stairs. It would seem that Lily had forgiven Max's transgressions with the serving girl. Though I couldn't tell for sure, Lily was very careful not to look in my direction while Max was in the room.

The morning and early afternoon passed in frenzied activity as everyone helped to decorate a tall spruce which was brought into the drawing room and positioned beside the piano. I luxuriated in the companionable attentions of Violet, but my heart sank as I watched the girls and their father playfully vie to hang favorite decorations on the tree. I would not let my brain even *form* the thoughts which seemed to squeeze the breath from me when Lloyd Beckwith whirled his wife around in an impromptu dance of celebration after the decorating was finished.

Once I caught Lily watching me with a quizzical expression on her pretty young face. She looked curiously from me to her mother, and my heart leaped to my throat as fears of unimaginable proportions claimed me. But the moment passed, and I commended myself on being able to go on breathing as if I were not just one big secret screaming to tell itself to the world.

Violet had asked me if I would do a watercolor sketch of her in the afternoon. My spirits soared at the prospect of being alone with her again so soon. She led me into her bedroom suite and disappeared into her dressing room while I set up an easel and readied my sketch box. I turned to find her sitting in a dark, high-backed chair by the flickering fireplace. She had removed every stitch of clothing and reclined against the claret-colored velvet upholstery in naked glory. I could scarcely get my breath.

"What if he — if someone comes . . . I mean what if Mr. Beck —" I stammered into silence, looking at her in shocked amazement.

"Oh, don't worry," she said offhandedly. "This sketch is to be a gift for him. He won't disturb us. I've asked him to join us when you are finished . . . Do you mind?"

Mind? What a strangely insignificant little word to describe what I felt. Of course I minded. I wanted him to *die*. To go away and be no part of her life . . . or mine. But I managed to shake my head and hide the fury that threatened to erupt in steam from my eyes and ears as from some evil and visible genie.

I threw my emotions into the creation at hand and soon had Violet's voluptuous likeness captured on the rough paper. My brushes flew from paint pot to water cup and back again. Delicate shadings and washes began to make her form move on the paper as if it lived on that flat plane as it did in the chair before me.

Finally I drew back and examined what I had done. It was truly my finest ever. My chest rose with pride and exhilaration as I crossed the room and took my beloved into my arms. She met my mouth with hers and squirmed her nakedness against my artist's smock in naughty revel as she pulled me into the space between her spread knees. She locked her legs around me just as I heard behind me the unmistakable sound of a door closing.

Lloyd Beckwith closed the few paces between us. I struggled to stand but Violet's legs around my waist held me fast against her.

"Shameless, Vi!" He stood with his legs apart and his hands on his hips. "You are truly without shame. You . . ." He pointed a finger close to my nose. "You have bewitched my wife."

I could not speak. My throat closed as if a collar had been pulled tight around my neck. Fear and shame thundered in my ears as comprehension flooded over me. My God. Discovered *flagrante delicto*. The worst of all possible events. On my knees between his wife's naked legs. I could feel the blood coming back to my face in a crimson rush. I closed my eyes and buried my face in my hands.

It was then I felt Violet struggling to rise. She released her grip on me and rose, pulling me to my unsteady feet as she did so. Her dark eyes flashed in anger as she shrugged into the robe her husband held out for her.

"Lloyd." She stepped toward him, tying the robe as she went. "How *could* you? I would have rung for you when we were ready."

He tossed his curls and raised his chin like a mischievous child. He came near to stamping a foot as he expressed his obvious impatience. "I *am* sorry, Vi, but the girls are clamoring to go caroling and you know I find it difficult to deny them — especially on holiday." He turned to the drying portrait on my easel pad and stroked his chin. He looked at me then. I mean to say he *truly* looked at me, studying me, it seemed. "My God," he said. "You *are* talented." He turned back to Violet. "Have you mentioned our proposal to your friend?"

Violet glanced at me with what I took to be a look of light chagrin. "No, Lloyd. I have not. But now that you have broached the subject, I certainly *will*." She came to me and took my hands in hers. I confess to emotions so mixed that I hardly knew how to react. "Sit down," she urged.

I gratefully sat, while both of them did the same. I had the feeling I supposed a deer might have when facing a hunter on one side and his dogs on the other.

Violet spoke softly then. I soon came to understand that she was asking me if I wanted to move away from Wellesley and live here at *The Maples* as her companion and tutor for her children. Lloyd, it seemed, had certain men friends with whom he spent much of his time, one of whom was his special friend. He and Violet enjoyed a marriage of amiable camaraderie, especially when they both spent time with their daughters.

Lloyd stood, hugged Violet to him, and then held her at arm's length. With warmth he said, "I have so wanted you to find someone worthy of you, and it seems now that you have." He included me in his embrace. I could not have been more shocked if he had suddenly levitated out the window.

He left the room in a rush of words and thrown kisses as youthful voices called from the hallway.

I looked at Violet with all my heart. That

evening we spent together the first of what would be
more than fifty Christmas eves. The holiday had
indeed brought a wealth of surprises and good
fortune.

FLASHPOINT by Katherine V. Forrest. 256 pp. Lesbian
blockbuster!   ISBN 1-56280-043-4 $22.95

CROSSWORDS by Penny Sumner. 256 pp. 2nd VictoriaCross
Mystery.   ISBN 1-56280-064-7   9.95

SWEET CHERRY WINE by Carol Schmidt. 240 pp. A novel of
suspense.   ISBN 1-56280-063-9   9.95

CERTAIN SMILES by Dorothy Tell. 160 pp. Erotic short stories
                                      ISBN 1-56280-066-3   9.95

EDITED OUT by Lisa Haddock. 224 pp. 1st Carmen Ramirez
Mystery.   ISBN 1-56280-077-9   9.95

WEDNESDAY NIGHTS by Camarin Grae. 288 pp. Sexy
adventure.   ISBN 1-56280-060-4   10.95

SMOKEY O by Celia Cohen. 176 pp. Relationships on the playing
field.   ISBN 1-56280-057-4   9.95

KATHLEEN O'DONALD by Penny Hayes. 256 pp. Rose and
Kathleen find each other and employment in 1909 NYC.
                                      ISBN 1-56280-070-1   9.95

STAYING HOME by Elisabeth Nonas. 256 pp. Molly and Alix
want a baby . . . or do they?   ISBN 1-56280-076-0   10.95

TRUE LOVE by Jennifer Fulton. 240 pp. Six lesbians searching for
love in all the "right" places.   ISBN 1-56280-035-3   9.95

GARDENIAS WHERE THERE ARE NONE by Molleen Zanger.
176 pp. Why is Melanie inextricably drawn to the old house?
                                      ISBN 1-56280-056-6   9.95

MICHAELA by Sarah Aldridge. 256 pp. A "Sarah Aldridge"
romance.   ISBN 1-56280-055-8   10.95

KEEPING SECRETS by Penny Mickelbury. 208 pp. A Gianna
Maglione Mystery. First in a series. ISBN 1-56280-052-3   9.95

THE ROMANTIC NAIAD edited by Katherine V. Forrest &
Barbara Grier. 336 pp. Love stories by Naiad Press authors.
                                      ISBN 1-56280-054-X   14.95

UNDER MY SKIN by Jaye Maiman. 336 pp. A Robin Miller
mystery. 3rd in a series.   ISBN 1-56280-049-3.   10.95

STAY TOONED by Rhonda Dicksion. 144 pp. Cartoons — 1st
collection since *Lesbian Survival Manual.*   ISBN 1-56280-045-0   9.95

CAR POOL by Karin Kallmaker. 272pp. Lesbians on wheels
and then some!   ISBN 1-56280-048-5   9.95

NOT TELLING MOTHER: STORIES FROM A LIFE by Diane
Salvatore. 176 pp. Her 3rd novel.   ISBN 1-56280-044-2   9.95

GOBLIN MARKET by Lauren Wright Douglas. 240pp. A Caitlin
Reece Mystery. 5th in a series.   ISBN 1-56280-047-7   9.95

LONG GOODBYES by Nikki Baker. 256 pp. A Virginia Kelly
mystery. 3rd in a series.   ISBN 1-56280-042-6   9.95

FRIENDS AND LOVERS by Jackie Calhoun. 224 pp. Mid-western
Lesbian lives and loves.   ISBN 1-56280-041-8   9.95

THE CAT CAME BACK by Hilary Mullins. 208 pp. Highly praised
Lesbian novel.   ISBN 1-56280-040-X   9.95

BEHIND CLOSED DOORS by Robbi Sommers. 192 pp. Hot, erotic
short stories.   ISBN 1-56280-039-6   9.95

CLAIRE OF THE MOON by Nicole Conn. 192 pp. See the movie —
read the book!   ISBN 1-56280-038-8   10.95

SILENT HEART by Claire McNab. 192 pp. Exotic Lesbian
romance.   ISBN 1-56280-036-1   9.95

HAPPY ENDINGS by Kate Brandt. 272 pp. Intimate conversations
with Lesbian authors.   ISBN 1-56280-050-7   10.95

THE SPY IN QUESTION by Amanda Kyle Williams. 256 pp. 4th
Madison McGuire.   ISBN 1-56280-037-X   9.95

SAVING GRACE by Jennifer Fulton. 240 pp. Adventure and
romantic entanglement.   ISBN 1-56280-051-5   9.95

THE YEAR SEVEN by Molleen Zanger. 208 pp. Women surviving
in a new world.   ISBN 1-56280-034-5   9.95

CURIOUS WINE by Katherine V. Forrest. 176 pp. Tenth
Anniversary Edition. The most popular contemporary Lesbian
love story.   ISBN 1-56280-053-1   9.95

CHAUTAUQUA by Catherine Ennis. 192 pp. Exciting, romantic
adventure.   ISBN 1-56280-032-9   9.95

A PROPER BURIAL by Pat Welch. 192 pp. A Helen Black
mystery. 3rd in a series.   ISBN 1-56280-033-7   9.95

SILVERLAKE HEAT: A Novel of Suspense by Carol Schmidt.
240 pp. Rhonda is as hot as Laney's dreams. ISBN 1-56280-031-0   9.95

LOVE, ZENA BETH by Diane Salvatore. 224 pp. The most talked
about lesbian novel of the nineties!   ISBN 1-56280-030-2   9.95

A DOORYARD FULL OF FLOWERS by Isabel Miller. 160 pp.
Stories incl. 2 sequels to *Patience and Sarah.*   ISBN 1-56280-029-9   9.95

MURDER BY TRADITION by Katherine V. Forrest. 288 pp. A
Kate Delafield Mystery. 4th in a series.   ISBN 1-56280-002-7   9.95

THE EROTIC NAIAD edited by Katherine V. Forrest & Barbara Grier.
224 pp. Love stories by Naiad Press authors.   ISBN 1-56280-026-4   12.95

DEAD CERTAIN by Claire McNab. 224 pp. A Carol Ashton
mystery. 5th in a series.   ISBN 1-56280-027-2   9.95

CRAZY FOR LOVING by Jaye Maiman. 320 pp. A Robin Miller
mystery. 2nd in a series.   ISBN 1-56280-025-6   9.95

STONEHURST by Barbara Johnson. 176 pp. Passionate regency
romance.   ISBN 1-56280-024-8   9.95

INTRODUCING AMANDA VALENTINE by Rose Beecham.
256 pp. An Amanda Valentine Mystery. First in a series.
                                                ISBN 1-56280-021-3   9.95

UNCERTAIN COMPANIONS by Robbi Sommers. 204 pp.
Steamy, erotic novel.   ISBN 1-56280-017-5   9.95

A TIGER'S HEART by Lauren W. Douglas. 240 pp. A Caitlin
Reece mystery. 4th in a series.   ISBN 1-56280-018-3   9.95

PAPERBACK ROMANCE by Karin Kallmaker. 256 pp. A
delicious romance.   ISBN 1-56280-019-1   9.95

MORTON RIVER VALLEY by Lee Lynch. 304 pp. Lee Lynch at
her best!   ISBN 1-56280-016-7   9.95

THE LAVENDER HOUSE MURDER by Nikki Baker. 224 pp. A
Virginia Kelly Mystery. 2nd in a series.   ISBN 1-56280-012-4   9.95

PASSION BAY by Jennifer Fulton. 224 pp. Passionate romance,
virgin beaches, tropical skies.   ISBN 1-56280-028-0   9.95

STICKS AND STONES by Jackie Calhoun. 208 pp. Contemporary
lesbian lives and loves.   ISBN 1-56280-020-5   9.95

DELIA IRONFOOT by Jeane Harris. 192 pp. Adventure for Delia
and Beth in the Utah mountains.   ISBN 1-56280-014-0   9.95

UNDER THE SOUTHERN CROSS by Claire McNab. 192 pp.
Romantic nights Down Under.   ISBN 1-56280-011-6   9.95

RIVERFINGER WOMEN by Elana Nachman/Dykewomon.
208 pp. Classic Lesbian/feminist novel.   ISBN 1-56280-013-2   8.95

These are just a few of the many Naiad Press titles — we are the oldest and largest lesbian/feminist publishing company in the world. Please request a complete catalog. We offer personal service; we encourage and welcome direct mail orders from individuals who have limited access to bookstores carrying our publications.